The Ex Games

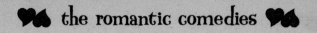
the romantic comedies

The Ex Games

JENNIFER ECHOLS

Simon Pulse

New York London Toronto Sydney

SIMON PULSE
An imprint of Simon & Schuster Children's Publishing Division
1230 Avenue of the Americas, New York, NY 10020
First Simon Pulse paperback edition October 2009
Copyright © 2009 by Jennifer Echols
All rights reserved, including the right of reproduction in whole or in part in any form.
SIMON PULSE and colophon are registered trademarks of Simon & Schuster, Inc.
For information about special discounts for bulk purchases, please contact Simon & Schuster Special Sales
at 1-866-506-1949 or business@simonandschuster.com.
The Simon & Schuster Speakers Bureau can bring authors to your live event. For more information or to book an event contact the Simon & Schuster Speakers Bureau at 1-866-248-3049 or visit our website at www.simonspeakers.com.
Designed by Ann Zeak
The text of this book was set in Garamond 3.
Manufactured in the United States of America
10 9 8 7 6 5 4 3 2 1
Library of Congress Control Number 2009923186
ISBN: 978-1-4169-7846-6
ISBN: 978-1-4169-8538-9 (eBook)

For Amy

seat belt

(sēt′ belt) *n.* **1.** a trick in which a snow-boarder reaches across the body and grabs the board while getting air **2.** what Hayden needs to fasten, because Nick is about to take her for a ride

At the groan of a door opening, I looked up from my chemistry notebook. I'd been diagramming molecules so I wouldn't have any homework to actually take home. But as I'd stared at the white paper, it had dissolved into a snowy slalom course. The hydrogen and oxygen atoms had transformed into gates for me to snowboard between. My red pen had traced my path, curving back and forth, *swish, swish, swish,* down the page. I could almost feel the icy wind on my cheeks and smell the pine trees. I couldn't *wait* to get out of school and head for the mountain.

Until I saw it was Nick coming out the door of Ms. Abernathy's room and into the hall. At six feet tall, he filled the doorway with his model-perfect looks and cocky attitude. He flicked his dark hair out of his eyes with his pinkie, looked down at me, and grinned brilliantly.

My first thought was, *Oh no: fuel for the fire.* About a month ago, one of my best friends had hooked up with one of Nick's best friends. Then, a few weeks ago, my other best friend and Nick's other best friend had gotten together. It was fate. Nick and I were next, right?

Wrong. Everybody in our class remembered that Nick and I had been a couple four years ago, in seventh grade. They gleefully recalled our breakup and the resulting brouhaha. They watched us now for our entertainment value, dying to know whether we'd go out again. Unfortunately for them, they needed to stick to DVDs and Wii to fill up their spare time. Nick and I weren't going to happen.

My second thought was, *Ah, those deep brown eyes.*

Maybe snowboarding could wait a little longer, after all.

"Fancy meeting you here, Hoyden." He closed the door behind him, too hard. He must have gotten in trouble for talking again, and Ms. Abernathy had sent him out in the hall.

Join the club. From my seat against the cement block wall of our high school's science wing, I gazed up at him—way, *way* up, because I was on the floor—and tried my best to glare. The first time he'd called me *Hoyden*, years ago, I'd sneaked a peek in the dictionary to look up what it meant: a noisy girl. Not exactly flattering. Not exactly a lie, either. But I couldn't let him know I felt flattered that he'd taken the time to look up a word in the dictionary to insult me with. Because that would make me insane, desperate, and in unrequited love.

He slapped his forehead. "*Oh*, I'm sorry, I meant *Hayden*. I get confused." He had a way of saying *oh* so innocently, like he had no idea he'd insulted me. Sometimes new girls bought his act, at least for their first few weeks at our school. They were taken by the idea of hooking up with Nick Krieger, who occasionally was featured in teen heart-throb magazines as the heir to the Krieger Meats and Meat Products fortune. And Nick obliged these girls—for a few dates, until he dumped them.

I knew his pattern all too well. When I'd first moved to Snowfall, Colorado, I had *been* one of those girls. He'd made me feel like a princess for a whole month. No, better—like a cool, hip teenage girl who dated! The fantasy culminated with one deep kiss shared in the back row of the movie theater with half our English class watching us. It didn't end well, thus the aforementioned brouhaha.

I blinked the stars out of my eyes. "Fancy seeing *you* here, Ex."

He gave me his smile of sexy confidence, dropped his backpack, and sank to the floor beside me. "What do you think of Davis and Liz?"

My heart had absolutely no reason to skip a beat. He was *not* asking me out. He was asking me my opinion of my friend Liz and his friend Davis as a couple. That did not necessarily mean he was heeding pub-lic opinion that he and I were next to get together. Liz and Davis were a legitimate topic of gossip.

I managed to say breezily, "Oh, they'll get along great until they discuss where to go on a date. Then he'll insist they go where she wants to go. She'll insist they go where *he* wants to go. They'll end up sitting in her driveway all night, fighting to the death over who can be more thoughtful and polite."

Nick chuckled, a low rumble in his chest. Because he'd sat down so close to me and our arms were touching, sort of, under layers and layers of clothing, I felt the vibration of his voice. But again, my heart had no reason—repeat, *no* reason—to skip two beats, or possibly three, just because I'd made Nick laugh. He made everybody feel this good about their stupid jokes.

"And what's up with Gavin and Chloe?" he asked next.

"Chloe and Gavin are an accident waiting to happen." I couldn't understand this mismatch between the class president and the class bad boy, and it was a relief finally to voice my concerns, even if it *was* to Nick. "They're both too strong-willed to make it together long. You watch. They're adorable together now, but before long they'll have an argument that makes our tween-love Armageddon look like a happy childhood memory."

Suddenly it occurred to me that I'd said way too much, and Nick would likely repeat this unflattering characterization to Gavin, who would take it right back to Chloe. I really did hold this opinion of Chloe and Gavin's chances at true love, but I'd never intended to share it! I lost my inhibitions when I looked into Nick's dark eyes, damn him.

I slid my arm around him conspiratorially—not as titillating as it sounds, because his parka was very puffy—and cooed, "But that's just between you and me. I know how good you are at keeping secrets."

He pursed his lips and gazed at me reproachfully for throwing our seventh-grade history in his face, times two. Back then he'd brought our tween-love Armageddon on himself by letting our whole class in on his secret while he kept me in the dark.

Not that I was bitter.

But instead of jabbing back at me, he slipped his arm around me, too. And I was *not* wearing a puffy parka, only a couple of T-shirts, both of which had ridden up a little in the back. I knew this without looking because I felt the heat of his fingers on my bare skin, above the waistband of my jeans. My face probably turned a few shades redder than my hair.

"Now, Hoyden," he reprimanded me, "Valentine's Day is a week from tomorrow. We don't want to ruin that special day for Gavin and Chloe or Davis and Liz. We should put aside our differences for the sake of the kids."

I couldn't help bursting into unladylike laughter.

I expected him to remove his hand from my hip in revulsion at my outburst, but he kept it there. I knew he was only toying with me, I *knew* this, but I sure did enjoy it. If the principal had walked by just then and sensed what I was thinking, I would have gotten detention.

"Four years is a long time for us to be separated," he crooned. "We've both had a chance to think about what we really want from our relationship."

This was true. Over the four years since we'd been together, I'd come to the heartbreaking realization that no boy in my school was as hot as Nick, nobody was as much fun, and nobody was nearly as much of an ass. For instance, he'd generated fire-crotch comments about me as I passed his table in the lunchroom yesterday.

Remember when another heir called a certain red-haired actress a fire-crotch on camera? No? Well, *I* remember. Redheads across America sucked in a collective gasp, because we *knew*. The jokes boys made to us about Raggedy Ann, the Wendy's girl, and Pippi Longstocking would finally stop, as we'd always hoped, only to be replaced by something infinitely worse.

So when I heard *fire-crotch* whispered in the lunchroom, I assumed it was meant for me. Nick was the first suspect I glanced at. His mouth was closed as he listened to the conversation at the lunch table. However, when there was commentary around school about me, Nick was always in the vicinity. He might not have made the comment, but I knew in my heart he was responsible.

Now I chose not to relay my thoughts on our four-year-long trial separation, lest he take his warm hand off my hip. Instead, I played along. "Are you saying you didn't sign the papers, so our divorce was never finalized?"

8

"I'm saying maybe we should call off the court proceedings and try a reconciliation." A strand of his dark hair came untucked from behind his ear, and he jerked his head back to swing the hair out of his eyes. Oooh, I *loved* it when he did that! I had something of a Nick problem.

His hair fell right back into his eyes. Sometimes when this happened, he followed up the head jerk with the pinkie flick, but not this time. He watched me, waiting for me to say something. Oops. I'd forgotten I was staring at him in awe.

A reconciliation? He was probably just teasing me, as usual. But what if this was his veiled way of asking me on a date? What if he was feeling me out to see whether I wanted to go with him before he asked me directly? This was how Nick worked. He had to win. He never took a bet that wasn't a sure thing.

And if he'd been listening to everyone in class prodding him to ask me out, the timing was perfect, if I did say so myself. He was between girlfriends (not that I kept up with his dating status) and therefore free to get together with me. Everett Walsh, my boyfriend of two months, had broken up with me last week because his mama thought I was brazen (no!). Therefore I was free to get together with Nick.

Playing it cool, I relaxed against the wall and gave his puffy parka a squeeze, which he probably couldn't feel through the padding. With my other hand, I found his fingers in his lap and touched the engraving on his signet ring, which he'd told me back in seventh grade was the Krieger family crest. It depicted blood-thirsty lions and the antlers of the hapless deer they'd attacked and devoured—which seemed apt for our relationship in seventh grade, but *not* for our relationship now, in eleventh. I was no deer in the headlights. Not anymore. Coyly I said, "I'll mention it to my lawyer." Ha!

He eyed me uneasily, like I was a chemistry lab experiment gone awry and foaming over. But Nick was never truly uneasy. He was just taken aback that I hadn't fallen at his feet. Then he asked, "What are you doing for winter break?"

Winter break was next week. We lived in a ski resort town. It seemed cruel to lock us up in school the *entire* winter. They let us out for a week every February, since the base might or might not start to melt by spring break in April.

Was he just making convo, whiling away our last few minutes of incarceration at school, or did he really want to know what I was doing during our days off? Again I got the distinct and astonishing impression that he wanted to ask me out. Perhaps I should notify Ms. Abernathy of a safety hazard in her chemistry classroom. Obviously I had inhaled hallucinatory gas just before she kicked me out.

"I'm boarding with my brother today," I said, counting on my fingers. "Tomorrow I'm boarding with Liz. Actually, Liz skis rather than boards, but she keeps up with me pretty well. I'm boarding with some friends coming from Aspen on Sunday, the cheerleading squad on Monday—"

Nick laughed. "Basically, anyone who will board with you."

"I guess I get around," I agreed. "I'm on the mountain a lot. Most people get tired of boarding after a while, which I do not understand at *all*. And then on Tuesday, I've entered that big snowboarding competition."

"Really!" He sounded interested and

surprised, but his hand underneath my hand let me know he was more interested in throwing me into a hot tizzy than in anything I had to say. He slid his hand, and my hand with it, from his lap and over to my thigh. "You're going off the jump? Did you get over your fear of heights?"

So he'd been listening to me after all.

My friends knew I'd broken my leg rappelling when I was twelve. That actually led, in a roundabout way, to my family's move from Tennessee to Colorado. My dad was a nurse, and he got so interested in my physical rehab that he and my mom decided to open a health club. Only they didn't think they could make it fly in Tennessee. The best place for a privately owned health club specializing in physical rehab was a town with a lot of rich people and broken legs.

Though my own leg had healed by the time we moved, I was still so shell-shocked from my fall that I never would have tried snowboarding if my parents hadn't made me go with my little brother, Josh, to keep him from killing himself on the mountain. Josh was a big part of the reason I'd gotten pretty good. *Any* girl would get pretty good trying to keep up with a boy snowboarder three years younger who was half insane.

And that's how I became the world's only snowboarder with the ability to land a frontside 900 in the half-pipe *and* with a crippling fear of heights. Not a good combination if I wanted to compete nationally.

"This competition's different," I said. Growing warmer, I watched Nick's fingers massaging the soft denim of my jeans. "For once, the only events are the slalom and the half-pipe. No big air or slopestyle or anything that would involve a jump. Chloe and Liz swore they'd never forgive me if I didn't enter this one."

"You've got a chance," Nick assured me. "I've seen you around on the slopes. You're good compared with most of the regulars on the mountain."

I shrugged—a small, dainty shrug, not a big shrug that would dislodge his hand from my hip and his other hand from my thigh. "Thanks, but I expect some random chick from Aspen to sweep in and kick my ass." And when that happened, I sure could use someone to comfort me in the agony of defeat, *hint hint*. But Nick was only toying with me. Nick was only toying with me. I could repeat this mantra a million times in my head, yet no matter how strong my willpower, his fingers rubbing across my jeans threatened to turn me into a nervous gigglefest. Sometimes I wished I were one of those cheerleaders/prom queens/ rich socialite snowbunnies who seemed to interest Nick for a day or two at a time. I wondered if any of them had given in to Nick's fingers rubbing across their jeans, and whether I would too, if he asked.

"Anyway, those are all my plans so far," I threw in there despite myself. What I meant was: I am free for the rest of the week, *hint hint*. I wanted to kick myself.

"Are you going to the Poser concert on Valentine's Day?" He eased his hand out from under mine and put his on top. His fingers massaged my fingers ever so gently.

Nick was only toying with me. Nick was only toying with me. "That's everybody's million-dollar question, isn't it?" I said. "Or rather, their seventy-two-dollar question. I don't want to pass up a once-in-a-lifetime opportunity to see Poser, but tickets are so expensive." I may have spoken a bit too loudly so he could hear me over my heart, which was no longer skipping beats. It was hammering out a beat faster than Poser's drummer.

Nick nodded. "Especially if you're buying two because you want to ask someone to go with you."

I gaped at him. I know I did. He watched me with dark, supposedly serious eyes while I gaped at him in shock. Was he laughing at me inside?

We both started as the door burst open. Ms. Abernathy glowered down at us with her fists on her hips. "Miss O'Malley. Mr. Krieger. When I send you into the hall for talking, you do not *talk* in the *hall*!"

"*Oh*," Nick said in his innocent voice.

I was deathly afraid I would laugh at this if I opened my mouth. I absolutely could not allow myself to fall in love with Nick all over again. But it was downright impossible to avoid. He bent his head until Ms. Abernathy couldn't see his face, and he winked at me.

Saved by the bell! We all three jumped as the signal rang close above our heads. On a normal day the class would have flowed politely around Ms. Abernathy standing in the doorway. They might even have waited until she moved. But this bell let us out of school for winter break. Ms. Abernathy got caught in the current of students pouring out of her classroom and down the hall. If she floated as far as the next wing, maybe a history teacher would throw her a rope and tow her to safety.

Chloe and Liz shoved their way out of the room and glanced around the crowded hall until they saw me against the wall on the floor. Clearly they were dying to know whether I'd survived being sent out in the hall with my ex. Both of them focused on the space between me and Nick. I looked down in confusion, wondering what they were staring at.

Nick was still holding my hand.

I tried to pull my hand away. He squeezed even tighter. I turned to him with my eyes wide. What in the world was he thinking? After the insults Nick and I had thrown at each other in public over the years, we would have been the laughing-stock of the school if we *really* fell for each other.

And now he was holding my hand in public!

He wouldn't look at me, though I pulled hard to free myself from his grasp. He just squeezed my hand and grinned up at the gathering crowd like he didn't care who saw us.

Which was *everyone*. Davis sauntered out of the classroom and slid his arm around Liz. Unlike the train wreck that was Chloe and Gavin as a couple, Liz and Davis were the two kindest people I knew. They deserved each other, in a good way. But even Davis had a comment as he casually glanced down at Nick and me and did a double take at our hands. "That's something you don't see every day," he understated to Liz. "Usually at about this time, Nick is going around the lab, collecting whatever particulate has dropped out of the solution so he can throw it at Hayden."

"We didn't do an experiment today, just diagrammed molecules. Nothing to throw," Nick said in a reasonable tone, as if he and I were not sitting on the floor, surrounded by a two-deep crowd of our classmates. They had all filed out of chemistry class and joined the circle. They peeked over one another's shoulders to see what Nick and I were up to this time.

Then Gavin exploded out of the classroom, and I knew Nick and I were in trouble. He whacked into Chloe so hard, he would have knocked her off her feet if he hadn't grabbed her at the same time. Over her squeals, he yelled at Nick, "I knew it!" while pointing at our hands.

"Oooooh," said the crowd, shifting closer around us, totally forgetting they were supposed to be *going home* for *winter break*. If Davis, Liz, Gavin, and Chloe hadn't made up the front row, the rest of the class would have overrun us like zombies.

"I was just shaking Hayden's hand, wishing her luck in the snowboarding competition Tuesday." Nick stood, still gripping my hand, pulling me up with him.

"See you tonight," Davis mouthed in Liz's ear. Then he turned to Nick and said, "Come on. I'll fill you in on what Ms. Abernathy said after you got ejected from the game." Of course Nick didn't give a damn what Ms. Abernathy said in the last ten minutes of class before winter break. But that was Davis, always smoothing things over.

Nick *finally* let go of my hand. "See you around, Hoyden." He pinned me with one last dark look and a curious smile. Then he and Davis made their way through the crowd, shoving some of the more obnoxious gawking boys, who elbowed them back.

But a few folks still stared at me: Liz, Chloe, and worst of all, Gavin. One corner of his mouth turned up in a mischievous grin. Gavin was tall, muscular, and Japanese, with even longer hair than Nick. I would have thought he was adorable if I didn't want to kill him most of the time for constantly goading Nick and me about each other. I certainly understood what Chloe saw in him, even though he drove her crazy too.

Gavin turned to her. "Give me some gum."

"No."

Liz and I dodged out of the way as Gavin backed Chloe against the lockers and shoved both his hands into the front pockets of her jeans. You might think the class president would find a way to stop this sort of manhandling, but actually she didn't seem to mind too much.

By now the crowd had dispersed. Nick and Davis were walking down the hall together, getting smaller and smaller until

I couldn't see them anymore past a knot of freshman girls squealing about the Poser concert and how they were working extra shifts at the souvenir shop to pay for the expensive tickets. Go home, people. I resisted the urge to stand on my tiptoes for one more peek at Nick. If I didn't run into him on the slopes, this might be the last I saw of him for ten whole days.

"I don't have any gum!" Chloe squealed through fits of giggling, trying to push Gavin off. "Gavin!" She finally shoved him away.

He jogged down the hall to catch up with Nick and Davis, holding the paper-wrapped of gum aloft triumphantly.

"That was my last piece!" Chloe called.

I never would have admitted that Gavin's gum theft made me jealous. Nick was bad for me, I knew. He was the last person on earth I wanted to steal my gum. Still, I stepped to one side so I could see him behind the Poser fangirls. I watched him turn with Gavin and Davis and disappear down the stairs, and I couldn't help but feel like a little kid on Halloween night, standing in the doorway in my witch costume with my plastic cauldron for trick-or-treat candy, watching the rain come down. Such sweet promise, and now I was out of luck. Damn.

Chloe stared after the boys too. I assumed she really wanted that gum. Then she looked at me. "Oh my God, did Nick ask you out? It sounded like he was asking you out, but we couldn't quite tell. Ms. Abernathy finally came to check on you because the whole first row got up from their desks and pressed their ears to the door."

I answered honestly. "For a second there, I thought he was going to ask me out."

"But he didn't?" Liz wailed.

To hide my disappointment, I bent down to stuff my chemistry notebook into my backpack as I shook my head.

"At least you got a *see you around*," Chloe pointed out. "Normally if he bothered to say good-bye to you at all, he would do it by popping your bra."

"True," I acknowledged. And then I realized what was going on here. Chloe and Liz had been hinting that I should go out with Nick now that they were dating Nick's friends, but at the moment they seemed even more eager and giddy about it than usual. I straightened, folded my arms across my chest, and glared at Chloe and then Liz. "Please do not tell me you put Nick up to asking me to the Poser concert."

Chloe stared right back at me. But Liz, the weakest link, glanced nervously at Chloe like they were busted.

"Come on now." I stamped one foot. "Even y'all aren't going to the Poser concert with Gavin and Davis. It's too expensive."

"Nick has more money than God," Chloe pointed out.

I turned on Liz. "You really want me to go out with him after I told you he made that fire-crotch comment about me?" Liz was all about people being respectful of one another. We were in school with teenage boys and this was asking a lot, I know.

"That *did* sound disrespectful," she admitted. "Are you sure he didn't mean it in a friendly way?"

Incredible. Even Liz's sense of chivalry and honor was crushed under the juggernaut called Wouldn't It Be Cute/Ironic If Nick and Hayden Dated Again.

"What if he *did* ask you out?" Liz bounced excitedly, and her dark curls bounced with her. "Oh my God, what if you saw him on the slopes over the break and he asked you to the Poser concert? What would you say?"

I considered this. Part of me wanted to think Nick had changed in the past four years. I would jump at the chance to go out with the boy I'd made up in my head. In real life Nick was adorable, funny, and smart, but in my fantasies he had the additional fictional component of honestly wanting to go out with me.

Another part of me remembered his dis four years ago as freshly as if it were yesterday. When I recalled that awful night, the image of Honest Nick dissolved, even from my imagination. That Nick was too good to be true. I couldn't say yes to Nick, because I was scared to death he would hurt me again.

"It doesn't matter," I declared, "because he's not going to ask me out. If he really liked me, he wouldn't have treated me the way he did back in the day. So stop trying to throw us together."

"Okay," Liz and Chloe said in unison. Again, too eager, too giddy. The three of us turned and made our own way down the hall.

We discussed how low Poser tickets would have to go before we sprung for them, but the subject had changed too easily. I was left with the nagging feeling that, despite their promise, they were not through playing Cupid with me and Nick.

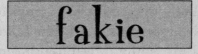

fakie

(fā′ kē) *n.* **1.** a trick performed in the stance opposite the one natural for the snow-boarder **2.** a trick performed by Nick on Hayden

I know what you're thinking. Girlfriend has fallen out of the stoopid tree and bonked her head against every branch on the way down. If Nick had such beautiful dark eyes and a low, rumbly voice and a perfect ass (did I mention his ass?) then why would I hold a grudge for something he did in the seventh grade?

Well, there was no mortification like seventh-grade mortification—just like my mom said there was no hunger like pregnancy hunger. Normal people got hungry, but pregnant women were driven toward food like starving wild animals, and a Big Mac never tasted so decadent to anyone. Clearly my mother had completed her research on this topic way before I broke my leg and my family turned health-conscious and vegetarian.

Not that I planned to find out about pregnancy hunger myself before I turned thirty. I had too much snowboarding to do first. But I was an expert on seventh-grade mortification. At that age you already worried that every step you took and every word out of your mouth would send your so-called "friends" into fits of laughter, because they hadn't quite outgrown the cruelty peculiar to sixth graders. If something truly mortifying happened to you on top of this, your heart began to shrink. And if, in addition, you were the new girl at school who wanted desperately to fit in, then in eleventh grade you would still be mad.

I moved to Snowfall about this time of year, terrified I'd make some blunder and everyone would hate me for the rest of middle school and high school. Or that these strangers would hear about the broken leg I'd just completed rehab for and would view me as the crippled girl and feel sorry for me, just like the kids did back in Tennessee. *Snowfall*—funny name for a ski resort town, at least the falling part. It made me worry I would take my dog for a walk one afternoon and slip into an icy crevice, never to be heard from again. The only evidence that I'd ever existed would be Doofus the Irish setter, trotting happily home, dragging his leash.

Instead, the opposite happened. Seconds after I handed my enrollment slip to the teacher and snuck into an empty desk in the back of English class, Nick picked up his books and moved to the desk beside mine.

I remembered every detail of that first five minutes with him, as if each minute were packed with a whole day's worth of emotion and color. Even back then, Nick was a head taller than most of the other boys in the class, and *so* handsome. He looked vaguely familiar in a way I couldn't quite place.

But what struck me most was how comfortable he seemed with me. The thirteen-year-old boys I'd known in Tennessee were split down the middle: Either they wouldn't make eye contact because they weren't interested in girls yet and played way too much Nintendo, or they were interested in girls and expressed this by making comments about their boobs. Unlike those immature boys, Nick talked to me as if we were friends. And he was funny. And he was hot. And I was the vulnerable new girl. I never had a chance.

Back then we weren't very mobile, of course. A seventh-grade "date" looked exactly like every other seventh grader's weekend outing: pizza at Mile-High Pie, the dive for locals only, and then whatever movie was playing at the theater down the street. Only, if you were on a little baby "date," you did all this while hanging with a boy, and the rest of the seventh-grade girls gazed at you in awe. And if your relationship were truly serious, you sat in the back row of the theater and kissed. I went on three "dates" with Nick, with no macking so far. The girls in my class squealed every time they saw me, beside themselves over the possibility that our fourth time might be sealed with a kiss.

On that fourth date, Mile-High Pie was packed with teenagers wearing hip winter sports gear even if they didn't ski or board. February in Tennessee was cold and brown, but Snowfall sparkled with excitement at the height of the ski season, like a beach town in summertime. I sat in a booth with Nick, surrounded by colored lights twinkling in the windows and decades of teen graffiti layered on the walls: VIOLET LOVES RANDY. ZACH + KAREN. That's what Nick and I were: Nick + Hayden. He watched me attentively, smiled at me, laughed at my jokes, and ignored Gavin elbowing him.

After a while we moved with the teenage crowd to the movie theater. Do you remember a Will Smith romantic comedy about a player who makes all the right moves to sneak into a woman's heart? IRONY. Maybe you could tell me the details sometime, because I wasn't paying much attention.

A tall, beautiful blonde named Chloe, obviously the prima donna of the class, was having a very public argument with two different boys who liked her. Because I was new, I had a hard time puzzling it out. There was a lot of high drama before the film started, middle schoolers yelling accusations at each other, like a Disney Channel version of *COPS*, and Chloe was comfortable at the center of it. I thought the attention had finally moved away from Nick and me, and we were safe from everyone's eyes in the back row.

The second the lights dimmed, he put his arm around me. We weren't wearing puffy parkas, either—we'd draped them over the backs of the seats when we'd come in—so the heat and weight of his arm imprinted themselves along my shoulders and the back of my neck. By the first love scene in the movie, he was leaning toward me.

I figured he wouldn't really kiss me. He would want to. He would mean to. But I couldn't possibly be lucky enough for this to happen for real, even though I *was* wearing my four-leaf clover earrings. The fire alarm would sound in the theater, or the roof would collapse under the weight of the snow. (I hadn't gotten used to two feet of snow blanketing everything.) The fact that we were hot for each other would be obvious to everyone, but like a pair of unfortunate saps on a TV sitcom, we wouldn't kiss for another two seasons.

And then he kissed me. His arm tightened around my shoulders, his other big hand cradled my cheek, and his warm lips touched mine. We kissed for a long time. I didn't make him stop. If this had happened in Tennessee, I would have known the boy just wanted to brag to his friends afterward. Nick made me think he honestly liked me and wanted to touch me.

My first kiss.

Obviously not his. He knew what he was doing.

I blink away tears thinking about this now. Such a perfect night, the sweetest reward after two years of embarrassment at school in Tennessee and excruciating pain 24/7. I'm feeling sorry for myself, I know, but I can't help crying for poor little thirteen-year-old me at the moment Nick kissed me. Because the castle in the air he'd built for me over the past month was about to come crashing down in the snow.

A girl named Liz bounced into the seat beside me and whispered that I should come to the bathroom with her and Chloe. This surprised me, because I'd never heard Liz's voice before—she was a quiet little librarian in class—and also because I'd begun to think no one dared disturb the mature teen bliss that Nick and I embodied. But I really did need to pee. I had needed to pee since the movie began. In seventh grade you do not admit to boys that you need to pee, so this was the perfect excuse to relieve myself while retaining my image as a peeless goddess.

When I came out of the stall, Chloe was peeking under the other doors to make sure the bathroom was empty. Liz stood in the center of the tiled room with her arms folded. I felt a flash of panic that maybe Colorado middle schools traditionally welcomed new students with a swirly. Or that Nick was on the list of boyfriends Chloe was balancing. I'd had my fun with him in the back row, and now she wanted payback. But Chloe didn't *look* bent on revenge. For the first time all month, she was silent, waiting, deferring to Liz.

By junior year Liz let her dark curly hair float around her shoulders. But back in seventh grade, she was still pulling it off her face with combs and clips with little monkey faces on them. The monkey faces laughed at me as she dropped the bomb. She told me Nick was from a famously rich family. Hadn't I seen the TV commercials last year in which Nick and his parents stood beside a huge rock fireplace and his father invited the camera to try Krieger Meats and Meat Products, from their family to yours?

That's why Nick looked familiar!

Liz said that at the beginning of the year, Nick and Gavin had argued about whether Nick's family money was the only reason he got any girl he wanted. So a month ago, when the English teacher let the class know a new girl was starting school, Nick bet Gavin he could get a date with the girl that weekend, sight unseen, without her knowing anything about his money. To make it fair, Nick and Gavin swore everyone in the class to secrecy.

I was not, as I'd thought, a cool teen. I was not Nick's dream girl. I was a bet.

And Liz and Chloe, feeling guilty, thought I should know. Now that Nick had kissed me, the bet had gone too far.

They also thought I would respond to this info by hugging them and crying in the bathroom, I'm pretty sure. They didn't expect me to flounce back into the theater and scream at Nick for what he'd done to me.

In the flickering light of the movie screen, he looked horrified. I held out hope that he would apologize and explain it was all a misunderstanding. Maybe I was a little starstruck after all. I couldn't believe the heir to the Krieger fortune had actually come on to me, even if his heart wasn't totally in it. He'd been so sweet to me for the past month. His kiss had felt real. I wanted him to like me for real.

After he'd gaped at me and I'd held my breath for a few moments, Gavin prompted him, "Well?"

Nick blinked and said in his faux-innocent voice, "I don't know what you're talking about, Hoyden. I mean, Hayden."

The theater burst into laughter, and *not* at Will Smith.

I stomped out. Liz and Chloe followed me, which sealed our friendship forever. Liz had told me what was up when no one else would, and Chloe was willing to leave her own intrigue behind, at least for the moment, to comfort me. We all trudged through the snow back to my house, made hot chocolate, and bitched about boys.

But the second the girls weren't looking, I escaped to my room, opened my dictionary, and looked up *hoyden*.

And here we still were. In the four years

since, every date I'd been on, every party, every school field trip, I remembered on two levels: how it went with my boyfriend at the time, and what Nick was doing in the background, with another girl, on the other side of the room or the other end of the bus. In other words, I was addicted to Nick.

Now the stage was set. I'd been boy-friendless for about a week, ever since the Incident with Everett Walsh's mama. Nick had dumped Fiona Lewis last week after three dates, which was one more date than he usually lasted in a relationship. I'd been watching him in class: *check*. I'd been dreaming about him at night: *check check*. He'd flirted with me in class for the past four years, but he'd never sat down with me in the hall and treated me to the low rumbly voice and hinted about the Poser concert. Now I wished I could resist him, especially since I suspected he'd started the fire-crotch discussion in the lunchroom on Thursday just to see if he could seduce me after insulting me. Exactly how easy was Hayden, anyway? Nick's inquiring mind wanted to know.

I was afraid he was about to find out. Despite myself, and despite Liz's lectures about disrespect, my blood raced through my veins every time I thought about his hand on my hand in the hall (not to mention my thigh). I didn't think I would answer yes if I ran into him during winter break and he asked me out. I *couldn't* answer yes. Still, I hoped against hope that he'd ask the question.

But I also hoped he'd wait until after Tuesday, because he was distracting me enough already. I had more important things to worry about than Nick. Tuesday I had an appointment with a snowboard.

I inhaled through my nose and felt my lungs fill with air. My blood spread the life-giving oxygen throughout my body.

I exhaled through my mouth and felt gravity pull the energy from my heart down through my legs, through my boots and snowboard, through the snow, to the rocks below. I was one with the mountain.

"Good luck, Hayden!" Liz squealed. I opened my eyes to find her in the crowd of spectators behind the ropes on one side of the snowy course. I spotted her right away because she was bouncing. Her dark curls flew into the eyes of people around her.

Chloe put one hand on Liz's shoulder to hold her down. "Hush, Hayden's doing one of her yoga things. Let her concentrate."

No chance of that now. Bouncing friends tended to break my concentration. At least my brother, Josh, and his friends weren't around. I'd checked in on them between my events, and all four of them were kicking butt in the fifteen-and-under boys' competition held on another course at the same time as my eighteen-and-under girls' contest. If they'd been here, they wouldn't have squealed like Liz. They would have made up a rap with beatboxing and very embarrassing pushing-up-the-house hand movements.

It's Hayden
What?
She's a maven
What?
On the ski slope
What?
Give it up, folks
What?
Got the board slide
What?
Got the frontside
What?
Got the mad skillz

What?
For a sick ride
What?

It was sad that I could predict their lyrics. I boarded with them *way* too much.

The warning buzzer sounded. In a few seconds I would begin my slalom run in my first-ever official competition. I'd run hundreds of casual races against friends and challenged my brother to comps in the half-pipe, but nothing like this. It was so strange to stand on my board as a competitor rather than as a spectator. I recognized the sensation of adrenaline bubbling through my veins. I felt it every time I stood behind the ropes and watched someone else start a slalom. The feeling was magnified by a thousand now that I didn't have to picture myself in the racer's place. I was really here.

And all because of Liz and Chloe. They'd told me I was good enough to compete. When I'd seen this competition advertised, I'd ignored it as usual. They'd pointed out to me that this one had no jump, nothing higher than the half-pipe wall, so I had no excuse not to try it. I wouldn't have been here without them. I winked at them on the sidelines, lowered my goggles, and slid my board forward to the starting line.

Deep breath. One with the mountain.

As a final touch, I twisted one of my four-leaf clover earrings. My dad had given them to me the day I got the cast off my leg, as an amulet for better luck in the future.

And then I was flying down the slalom course, staying tight and tucking in, dodging around the gates as fast as possible. I knew my time would be good because I was in the zone. My body went on automatic, feeling exactly what to do when. I enjoyed the bright sparkling day, the white snow, the spectators in crazy-colored gear lining both sides of the course, the too-blue sky. There was no feeling in the world like this, having a body that worked.

Then I hit my usual snag. For most people, the hardest part of this course was the moguls. For me, it was the straightaway past Nick's house. His parents' mansion had an enormous frontyard and a daunting front gate to scare away paparazzi and beggars. But the backyard bordered the slopes so the Kriegers could sit on their deck and watch the skiers. Every time I boarded past, no matter what trick I tried or who I was with,

I glanced over at the deck while attempting to look like I wasn't looking, just in case Nick was there. He never was.

Until now. I thought I couldn't feel any more adrenaline than was already pumping through my body in my first boarding competition ever. Apparently my body kept some adrenaline in reserve, because I flushed with a new rush at the realization that he was watching me. I could *not* let Nick distract me. It probably wasn't even him but his father. Or was it? I'd seen Mr. Krieger at my parents' health club. He had blond hair, not dark hair like Nick. And why would Mr. Krieger wear Nick's puffy parka?

Okay, Nick probably didn't recognize me from a distance. Though my red hair and hot-pink snowboard made me hard to miss. Okay, he might recognize me, but he hadn't *meant* to watch me. He was out on the deck to fetch a few more logs for the fire inside. The fact that he'd come outside at exactly the moment I took my turn in the competition was just a big coincidence. An almost impossible coincidence, actually.

Believe it or not, every bit of this flashed through my mind in one second.

My questions about Nick (*Is he looking at me? Is he looking at me on purpose? What does it meeeeeeeean???*) were familiar to me after four years. I had become very efficient. I thought them and then pushed them to the back of my mind before they made me fall down. I was one with the mountain. My body worked perfectly. I skimmed around the gates, torn between excitement that I could see the finish line and disappointment that I'd finished so fast. I always hated for a run to end.

I made a wide circle to slow down and skidded to a stop. Almost before the final curtain of snow I'd kicked up had fallen out of the sky, I was squinting at my time on the scoreboard.

"Holy shit," I whispered. I was in the lead! Three chicks waited to take their turns, but I was so far ahead of them after my half-pipe score, they'd have to really hightail it down the mountain to beat my overall score now.

What if I *won?* I'd dreamed about placing, but I'd never expected to *win!*

And then, so predictably that I wanted to hold myself down and rub my face with snow as punishment, I glanced way up the slope at Nick's deck to see if he was still watching me.

He was gone.

And *then* I heard the cheers and applause of the spectators for me, with Liz and Chloe's screams ringing above the noise even though they were near the top of the course, easing their way down through the crowd and the snow. I turned away from Nick's empty deck, unlatched my boots from my board, and hiked over to the sidelines to meet the girls. I had two friends who I knew for sure had come out to support me, and who weren't the least bit embarrassed to let everyone know it. They were the ones who were really important.

Besides, if I won this competition, I would be in big trouble, and Nick Krieger would be the least of my worries.

"So, what's next?" Liz asked the instant she plopped down beside me on the seat of the bus. "Are you registering tomorrow for that amateur comp in Aspen a couple of weeks from now?"

I'd been afraid of this. After the competition, Chloe had walked back to her parents' hotel. The bus would wind through the snowy streets from the ski resort to my house and then to Liz's. This ten-minute ride was my only chance to convince Liz to drop this idea of pushing me into more competitions, before she dragged Chloe onto the bandwagon with her.

I'd been so thrilled when Josh won third place in his boys' division. And I was absolutely ecstatic when the other times in my girls' division came in and I found out I'd WON THE WHOLE SHEBANG! It still hadn't quite sunk in. And now it never would. Because almost the second I realized I'd won, I started worrying about what came now.

"We already checked the Aspen contest," I reminded Liz, careful to keep my voice even. "It requires a big air event."

Liz spoke carefully too, using the fingertip of her glove to trace graffiti on the back of the bus seat, rather than looking at me. "Chloe and I thought that after you won the competition today—and we knew you would—you'd realize how good you are, and you'd start entering everything in sight."

"You and Chloe thought wrong." I stared past Liz's dark curly hair, out the bus window so streaked with salt that shops flashing by outside were just blurs of color.

"Let me put it this way," Liz said, looking directly at me now. "What am I doing after high school?"

"Getting a bachelor's in English from the University of Colorado and a master's in library science from the University of Denver," I recited. Liz and Chloe both had been very consistent in their career plans since I'd known them.

"And what's Chloe doing?" Liz prompted me.

"Going to Georgetown and getting into politics."

"And what are you doing?"

"Boarding," I muttered. I should have seen this convo coming, and now she'd backed me into a corner, even though I was sitting on the aisle.

"Unless you're planning on living with your parents forever, how are you going to board all day when you haven't gone pro? And how are you going pro when you won't enter any competitions to get there?"

She was right, of course. I'd known I would have to face this reality sooner or later. I wanted it to be later, after this year's snow season was over.

She persisted. "The prize for winning first place in the competition is lessons with Daisy Delaney, right?"

"Right." I felt myself grinning all over again at the thought. Daisy Delaney held a silver medal in the Olympics, an X Games title, and two world championships in women's snowboarding. Last December I got a big head after landing the 900, and I called the office of the Aspen slopes where she worked to inquire about lessons. I didn't want to miss an opportunity to develop in the sport if lessons with this stellar athlete were in my reach.

They weren't. The waiting list for lessons with her was three years long. And the cost was out of my league. But now I'd won this very prize: ten lessons with her.

"This is your opportunity to impress someone who can pull strings for you," Liz said. "I've heard of three Colorado girls Daisy Delaney's coached who've gone pro. But potential sponsors will want to photograph you snowboarding off a cliff. And after Daisy Delaney spends the morning drilling you on spins, she'll expect the two of you to leave the main slopes and shred the back bowls. You're not going to tell her, 'No thanks, I don't go off cliffs. Don't bother coaching me in slopestyle or big air, either, because I don't board off anything higher than my own head.'"

Liz was mocking me. *Liz*, who never said an unkind thing to anyone, was mocking *me*, one of her best friends! I gazed reprovingly at her and hoped my hurt look would shock her into an apology.

She folded her arms as best she could in her thick coat, and she raised her eyebrows at me under her dark curls and blue knitted hat. She was right again. Fear of heights would be a little hard to explain to a snowboarding coach who might want to take a chance on me.

I just didn't want to hear it.

The bus squealed to a stop, which snapped us out of our stare-down. We both glanced around and realized we'd reached my street. "We'll continue this discussion tonight," she told me in an authoritative voice, as if I didn't already have a mother.

"Give it a rest, would you, Liz?" I wailed. "I appreciate what you're doing, I really do. But Chloe invited us over tonight so we can celebrate my win. At least let me enjoy the thrill of victory, okay? We can talk about how it's ruined my life tomorrow."

As I stood, I saw Josh crouched in the seat behind us. I'd thought he'd sat in the back of the bus. Maybe he had, but then he'd worked his way up the aisle for eavesdropping. When we locked eyes and he realized he was busted, he dashed past me down the aisle as best he could in snowboarding boots and disappeared through the door.

"Oh God, there's been a security breach," I gasped to Liz. "See you tonight."

"See you," she sang after me, her authoritative tone totally gone. In fact, she sounded eager and giddy, just as she and Chloe had last Friday in the hall when we'd discussed Nick. I had a feeling she and Chloe were not going to leave my fear of heights alone.

And neither was Josh. I did my best to dash after him, clunking down the bus stairs into the crisp air. He'd already pulled his snowboard out of the rack on the side of the bus and was hiking up the icy sidewalk. I slid my own board from the rack and chased him. "Hey!" I hollered. "James Bond! What's the big idea?"

He stopped on the slick sidewalk and whirled around to face me. "You're supposed to take me with you," he snarled.

"Pardon?" I played dumb to put off the inevitable, because I had a good idea what he meant.

"That's what siblings do for each other, like Elijah and Hannah Teter, and Molly and Mason Aguirre. You're supposed to make it as a pro snowboarder, then reach back and help me do the same."

I stared blankly at him, waiting for him to acknowledge the irony of *him* scolding *me*, when I was older than him. I moved closer so I could stare down my nose at him. This didn't work. He was almost as tall as me. He'd shot up a few inches lately and was about to catch up to me. And he was standing above me on the sloped sidewalk.

His dark eyes were shaped like mine. He had a scattering of freckles like I did, but not as prominent, even though I tried to even mine out with makeup. And he used to have hair almost as bright red as mine, but now his hair was dark brown. Flashes of red echoed in the strands only when he moved his head in the sunlight reflecting off the snowdrifts in our neighbors' yards. He'd outgrown his red hair as easily as his peanut allergy. He actually wasn't bad-looking. Eventually he might even land his crush, Gavin's sister Tia. My hair, in contrast, was as red as the day I was born. As red as Shaun White's, the greatest snowboarder ever. Strangers on the slopes were always calling to me that I could be his little sister.

But I wasn't. "I'm no Hannah Teter," I insisted, "or Molly Aguirre, either."

"You *could* be," Josh insisted. "You're supposed to have a fear of heights for a little while after you break your leg. You're not supposed to have it *four years* after you start snowboarding. And you definitely can't let it ruin your chance of impressing Daisy Delaney. I'm not going to let you." He spun on the ice and stomped up the sidewalk again, dragging his board.

"What are you going to do, *tell* on me because I won a snowboarding contest?"

"That's exactly what I'm going to do," he called haughtily over his shoulder.

Uh-oh. I definitely did not want my parents butting into my business, especially not about this. "You had better not," I shouted after him. "Do you hear me, O'Malley? I will tell Gavin's sister you slept with a stuffed bunny rabbit until you were in middle school, so help me God!"

Josh dropped his board, slid down to me, and clamped his hand over my mouth. "Shhhh! Mr. Big Ears was very special."

It took me a full ten seconds to push Josh off me. I hoped no more buses passed by, because the tourists inside would probably grip the poles in the middle of the bus and edge a bit farther from the crazy locals. Last winter I would have beat Josh away with no problem. He was growing fast. I wouldn't be able to overpower him much longer, so we needed to solve this issue before then.

Avoidance was so much easier. I'd had enough of him and Liz both dragging me down in the midst of my happy afternoon. "Don't tell them," I said again between gasps. I bent his fingers backward to make him let me go.

"Ow!" he barked, rubbing his fingers, face bright red underneath his freckles. I shouldn't have bent his fingers back. This was another thing Josh and I had in common: a bad temper. We might seem good-natured to the point of ditsy, but push us too far and we'd snap. I was using yoga to work on this. Judging from our current convo, Josh was not.

He bent to snag his board and jogged up the slippery slope. He wanted to beat me home. What would he tell Mom when he got there?

"Josh!" I shouted, jogging after him as best I could. I tripped over my board and lost my grip. It zipped back down the sidewalk, past two houses, and crashed into a mailbox. At least I knew I'd done a good job of waxing it last night. I trotted after it and called pitifully to Josh as I picked it up. "Little bro, I love you so much!"

Way up the hill, he disappeared inside our house.

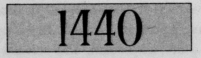

1440

(fôr tēn fôr′ tē) *n.* **1.** a quadruple spin, nearly impossible to pull off **2.** Hayden's fear of heights, nearly impossible to hide

When I finally made it into the mud room, panting with exertion and hot under five layers of clothing, Josh had only pulled off his boots. He sat on the bench and playfully grabbed at Doofus's snout. He hadn't spilled anything to Mom yet. Whew.

I extracted myself from my parka. "You are, seriously, my favorite brother."

Josh scratched Doofus's ears and seemed to be telling the dog rather than me, "I'm your *only* brother. And you bent my fingers back and hurt them." He poked out his bottom lip.

"I will kiss your fingers and make them better, kissy kissy," I threatened him. That got him up pretty quickly. He kicked off the rest of his snow clothes and skidded into the kitchen in his long johns and socks. I stripped down to my long johns, too—tripped over Doofus—and scrambled after Josh, angry already about what he might tell Mom, depending on how mischievous he felt.

Mom was giving him a big hug, wearing her yoga leotard from work, holding the large kitchen knife she'd just been chopping dinner with. If they weren't my family I might have been frightened. "Well, how'd you do?" she asked, pulling back to look him in the face.

"I won third place in the junior boys' division!" Josh exclaimed with wide, innocent eyes like an adorable woodland creature in a Disney cartoon. I wondered what he was up to. I wanted to slap him. But then I would be forced to explain to my mom why I'd slapped the adorable woodland creature.

"That's great, honey!" She wrapped him in another hug. He was facing me now. He gave me a wink and a thumbs-up. Ugh!

Mom eased out of the hug with him but kept her hands on his shoulders. "Why are you acting like a parody of yourself?" she asked him.

Josh blinked at her. "That's just a function of being a teenager. I feel so empty inside. What's for dinner?" He slipped out from under her hands and wandered to the refrigerator.

Mom turned to me, and the big grin she'd worn for Josh sagged a little. She didn't expect much from my first snowboard competition. "And how'd you do, honey?"

"I did okay."

"I'll give you five seconds," Josh called from behind the refrigerator door.

Mom looked at Josh, then back at me. "What? What is it?"

I looked into her eyes, dark like Josh's and mine. I took in her long red hair tamed into a braid down her back, her freckles that made her look younger than forty-six. At least, I thought so, and I hoped so, because clearly I was going to look just like her. Maybe she'd take my side, whatever Josh was about to tell her. She knew how hard my injury had been on me.

"Actually . . . ," I said slowly.

With each of my syllables, her right eyebrow arched higher.

"I won," I finished.

"Oh my God, that's great, you won!" With her braid bouncing as she jumped up and down, she looked and sounded a lot like Liz—except for, you know, the knife. "That means you're a lot better at snowboarding than I thought! You've finally gotten over your fear of heights! And—wait a minute—why didn't you want to tell me?" Abruptly she stopped jumping. "What's the prize?"

Josh walked over with a stalk of celery sticking out of his mouth. He took the knife from Mom's hand and set it on the counter. Then he said around the celery, "Lessons with Daisy Delaney."

"Daisy Delaney!" Mom gasped. "Hayden! I am old and out of it, as you're so fond of telling me, but even *I* know who Daisy Delaney is. That's some prize!"

"But guess what?" Josh went on, removing the celery from his mouth so he could rub this in as thoroughly as possible. "Hayden's been avoiding comps all this time because they have jumps in them. Her fear of heights is so bad that Daisy Delaney's going to think she's a beginner."

Mom turned back to me, and her other eyebrow went up. "Really?"

"She won't set foot on the gondola," Josh blathered on. "She won't even get on the regular ski lifts that go too high off the ground. She sticks to the low, short lifts, which means she's been boarding for four years and she's never even seen half the mountain."

"That half of the mountain is nothing but jumps and cliffs. I don't *want* to see it," I insisted.

"This is bullshit!" Josh shouted over me. "Mom, she's supposed to take me with her. Like Elijah and Hannah Teter. Like Molly and Mason Aguirre."

"Who?" Mom shouted back.

"One sibling goes pro and helps the other along." Josh gestured dramatically with the celery. "You could have *two* pro snowboarders in the family. We would buy you a new minivan. You want a new minivan, don't you?"

"Tempting," Mom told him drily. She turned and gave me a long look. "Well, Hayden? You've said you want to become a professional snowboarder, but your father and I assumed you wouldn't be able to do that because of your fear of heights. We thought eventually you'd give up, go to college, and major in . . ." Her voice trailed off.

And no wonder. Currently I had a C in chemistry, a C in history, and a D in algebra. Ms. Abernathy wasn't the only teacher sending me out in the hall for talking.

"But if you're good enough to win a contest in Snowfall," Mom went on, "and you have a foot in the door with Daisy Delaney, you have as good a chance of going pro as anybody. Do you want help getting over your fear of heights? We could take you to the doctor—"

"Yeah, that's just what I need, to miss my days snowboarding so I can sit in some doctor's office and go through more rehab." My voice rose and thinned until it petered out at the end, and *rehab* was a whisper. My fear of doctors might actually have been worse than my fear of heights, judging from my shallow breaths.

Mom must have noticed, because she put her hand on my shoulder. "Or a counselor of some kind?"

"Absolutely not."

"Don't let her get away with this." Josh pointed at my mother with the celery. "She is a foolish, foolish young girl."

Mom rolled her eyes at Josh. "Lay off her, would you? If she doesn't want help with her phobia, she'll work through it on her own, or she won't go pro. It's not something we can decide for her. Get your own lessons with Daisy Delaney. I'm going to call your father and tell him the good news. Where's my phone?" She padded out of the kitchen in her bare feet, braid swinging gently against her back. Then there was a screech and a dog yelp. She must have tripped over Doofus lying on the floor in the living room. "I'm okay," she called.

I was holding my breath. When I realized this and forced myself to breathe again, I smelled smoke. Mom had left dinner burning. I dashed to the stove to stir the tofu.

I didn't look at Josh, but out of the corner of my eye I could see him standing at the counter, stuffing his face with handfuls of organic rice crisps out of the bag. Finally I said, "You owe me."

"I don't owe you anything." He sidled

over and tried to stick a rice crisp in my ear. "You're supposed to take me with you. That's what siblings do."

I batted his hand away and shook the tofu-y spatula at him. "If I ever do go pro, I have no obligation to take you with me. Younger siblings have to earn that kind of favor. You *told* on me for winning a contest, you ass! You owe me. And you know what I want in return."

He scowled at me. "Not the pants."

I nodded gravely. "Give me your pants."

These were no magical traveling pants. They were only my little brother's broken-in jeans that fit me perfectly and that he almost never let me wear. I'd even tried on the identical size and style at the store, but they weren't the same.

He knew how I loved them, too, so he sabotaged them just to irk me. Once he tore a hole in the butt so my panties would show. This might have been an accident, but I was pretty sure the edges of the hole were cut, not frayed. I got revenge on him by patching up the hole with a little red heart. Infuriatingly he wore them like that out in public, as if I didn't have enough social problems without a little brother with hearts sewn onto his behind.

This time, as I stood in my bedroom and looked the jeans over, just in case, before pulling them on, I saw that he'd written BOY TOY in big block letters across the butt in permanent marker, right next to the heart patch. Never mind that *he* would have to wear them to school like that. It was worth it to him if he embarrassed *me*. Gah, he might have made it to the eighth grade, but he was still such a little brother! When we were fifty he'd still be stuffing my snow boots with wet macaroni.

But I had to wear the jeans tonight while I had the chance, and the marker would probably take years to wash out. That was okay. I enjoyed feeling like I looked good, but I wouldn't be trying to impress anyone with my outfit tonight. For winning the competition, Chloe and Liz were throwing me a "party" at Chloe's parents' hotel. What this really meant was that Chloe would suck face with Gavin, Liz would suck face with Davis, and I would keep the onion dip company. No one would notice my BOY TOY butt. It was sweet of Chloe and Liz to *intend* to celebrate my win and show me a good time, even if I knew it wouldn't work out that way.

So after dinner I rode the bus back into town, waved to the doorman at the front entrance of the hotel, and made my way downstairs into the kitchen adjoining the banquet room. A beautiful cake frosted with CONGRATULATIONS HAYDEN! waited on the counter, and a chick wailed lonely emo lyrics from the stereo. But the room was empty.

"Hello?" I called, my voice echoing above the music.

There was a scream, and then a door opened. Chloe stepped out of the pantry, smoothing her hands through her mussed blond hair. "Hey girl! Oh my God, you look so awesome in those jeans!"

"Thanks. Josh let me borrow them. You'll never see them again unless I find something else to coerce him with, but it'll be two years before he's old enough to drive down to Denver and buy crack."

"I'm serious." She looked me up and down. "You could be a model."

"Selling what? Hamburgers, like the Wendy's girl? I have red hair and freckles."

"Think about Lindsay Lohan."

"I'd rather not," I muttered as Chloe

turned me around backward and lifted up my coat to admire my ass.

Then she gasped. "Oh my God, 'boy toy'?"

"That's me, fast and loose." This came out sounding more wistful than I'd intended, and I hoped she didn't guess I was thinking about Nick. "Speaking of which, I take it you and Gavin are rearranging the soup cans?" I nodded toward the pantry.

"Ah . . . yeah." Her cheeks tinged pink. "We're almost through with our inventory."

"You *are*?" I exclaimed.

"I mean, that didn't come out right." She blushed more deeply. It was hilarious to see Chloe flustered, which happened only once a year or so. She must *really* like Gavin, which I still found bizarre.

"We'll be out in a sec," she said. "Liz and Davis are in the hot tub."

They certainly were. The back of the kitchen was a wall of windows overlooking the hotel's heated pool and hot tub. Steam rose from the water and wisped into the night. Over Chloe's shoulder I could see Liz and Davis deep in the hot tub, seeking refuge from the frigid winter air, kissing slowly. I didn't have the heart to interrupt. Knowing them, it had taken them half an hour to work up the courage to touch each other at all.

"No hurry." I winked to show Chloe my support for taking inventory with Gavin. It was very important that a winter resort hotel never run out of soup. She backed into the pantry and closed the door.

I examined my cake on the counter again. CONGRATULATIONS HAYDEN! The only thing worse than being abandoned at my own victory party was letting my friends know I cared about this, and making them feel bad about it so they stayed with me instead of stealing the alone-time they really wanted with their boyfriends. You know what it was like? It was exactly like being grateful to my friends in Tennessee for continuing to hang out with me when I was in a wheelchair, but knowing all along that they'd rather ditch me.

I missed Everett Walsh for the first time since we'd broken up last week.

Suddenly I realized I was staring at Liz and Davis again, his dark hand stroking her porcelain complexion. Okay, I would *not* stare at my friends making out like I was love-starved. From the hot tub my gaze traveled up, over the faux-rustic shops of downtown Snowfall and the white lights strung in the bare trees. The dark mountain looming over the town was visible in the night only because starlight reflected on the snowy slopes. I'd always regarded that mountain as my friend. It had given me years of highs induced by sun and speed. It had helped me regain so much of the confidence I'd lost when I'd broken my leg. Tonight, for the first time ever, the mountain looked cold and menacing. I shivered.

I knew one way to warm up, besides the hot tub and the pool. I hurried to the locker room to change into the bikini and flip-flops I'd brought to enjoy the hotel amenities. Then I dashed back through the cold banquet room. The door into the hallway squealed, letting anyone in the sauna know I was coming.

A few times over the years, Chloe and I had surprised hotel guests in compromising situations in the sauna. Tonight I might walk in on a beer-fueled boys' night out for a group of middle-aged men, in which case I would make an excuse and back out of the sauna. But now that the hallway door had developed this squeak, at least I knew I wouldn't interrupt folks in the middle of something they shouldn't be doing in a public place.

As I pushed open the sauna door and stepped into the eucalyptus-scented steam, I saw I wouldn't be alone. The other occupant had heard me coming and was wrapping his towel more modestly around his bathing suit. I could still back out of the small, dark space. I hesitated to slide onto the bench across from him until I got a good look at him.

I squinted through the mist and finally realized it was—"Nick! I mean, Ex!"

"Hayden! I mean, Hoyden!" He sounded as surprised to see me as I was to see him. His eyes slid to my bare tummy. "You have a body like a rock."

Right back at ya, I could have said. I'd known Nick was built. His family had a membership at my parents' health club, and sometimes he came in to lift weights. His favorites were the arm curl machine and the abdominal machine, where he would lift hard for long minutes and then fight for a few last painful crunches. Not that I made a habit of standing there and staring at him as he worked out. That would be creepy. I watched him on the surveillance cameras behind the reception desk.

Even though he never worked out with his shirt off, I could have predicted that what I saw now had been hiding under his tee: six-pack abs with beads of sweat sliding down them, like a disembodied torso in a workout machine infomercial. But I was surprised at how thin he was. There wasn't an ounce of fat on him anywhere. I watched the muscles of his upper arms move underneath his skin as he leaned forward and put his hands on his knees. I had the strange sensation I was seeing a different person, a real person, rather than the model-handsome perfection who had sashayed his way through my school and my fantasies for the last four years. Suddenly he was less a superhero and more a boy my age, caught off guard in the sauna.

I liked this Nick even better.

And *he* approved of *my* body, too.

Or did he? Did a girl want to be a rock? Was this a compliment? I draped my towel across the bench opposite him and sat down.

"What kind of rock?" I asked casually. "Granite is rough. Mica is shiny and flaky." Whoops. I was feeding him jokes. I might as well have sat there and insulted myself. Nick didn't even need to participate.

Both of those sound right, he would have said if we were trading insults across the chemistry classroom. Instead he said, "Come over here and give me a closer look."

Nick was hot, and his voice was honey. We were alone in a cloud of steam. I wanted so badly to close the five feet of space between us by hopping down from my bench and jumping onto his.

But there was no way. That's what I'd do if I were still the new girl at school who wasn't wise to him yet. I said, "You're the one who wants the look. *You* come over *here.*"

His gaze slid up my body to my face. His eyes locked with mine and held me there. Would he give in to this battle of wills? Or did he figure that if it led to contact with a girl, he always won?

Yeah, he sure was acting like he had the upper hand. Still holding me in place with his eyes, slowly he stepped down from his bench. He stepped up onto my bench and settled beside me on my towel. And he slid one hand onto the bare skin of my tummy.

I tried not to flinch. I told myself he didn't mean anything by it—he was just the school's biggest flirt—so there was no reason to make him unhand me. In fact, I'd found through experience that people who didn't flinch seemed to fare better with Nick, because he wasn't sure what to do with them. And I *had* told him to come over here.

Besides, it was just my tummy, my innocent tummy that I showed to the general public every summer at the pool. But Nick had never touched my bare tummy before, and my body screamed at me to *pay attention, this was serious,* just as when he'd touched my bare hip in the school hall last Friday. However dark and dangerous I'd considered Nick before, he was about to get a lot worse.

Or better. "The smooth white stone that statues are carved from," he clarified, brushing his warm fingertips across my skin. "Marble."

I did my best to keep my tummy absolutely still so he wouldn't feel how fast I was breathing. This required me to take very small breaths of heavy hot sauna air through my nose. No wonder what I said next sounded strained: "Marble? With black veins? Sounds attractive."

He smiled a little. "Statues don't talk."

"Yeah, I wasn't buying this sexy rock metaphor anyway."

His eyebrows went up and his face opened into that *who, me?* innocent expression of his, even as his pointer finger dipped inside my belly button. "I'm trying to be nice to you."

"I can tell." Something needed to be done about this belly button issue. I didn't push his hand away because . . . well . . . I wanted it there. But I couldn't just leave it there without acknowledging it, either. That would show weakness, telling Nick he could do whatever he wanted with me and I would just sit there and take it. That would be every girl he'd ever dated. Instead, I put my hand on top of his and pressed gently, like I approved.

Which I did.

I think I surprised him. Oooh, I *loved* this! His nostrils flared a little, and his big hand under my hand spread all the way across my tummy, stroking there slowly. Something was definitely going to happen, and I was going to let it.

But while he was off balance, I needed information from him. Now that I'd gotten over the surprise of seeing him at Chloe's hotel, it occurred to me just how out of place he was. "What are you doing here?"

"Chloe invited me."

"She *did?*" I squeaked. I hoped he didn't assume I'd put her up to it. I *knew* I couldn't trust Chloe and Liz to quit the Cupid business!

For once, being a very bad actress served me well. Nick could see I was floored by this info. He explained, "Chloe asked Gavin to invite me to your victory party. Didn't they tell you?"

"I didn't see Gavin," I said slowly, still puzzling this out. "I only talked to Chloe for a minute. I don't think they know you're here."

"Maybe they don't," he admitted. "I came in and saw Davis and Liz making out in the hot tub, and I heard these groans coming from the pantry. What are Gavin and Chloe doing in there anyway?" he asked in his *I'm so innocent* voice.

I laughed. "Chloe said they were taking inventory."

Nick chuckled. "Gavin wishes. Last I heard, he had no idea how many boxes of cereal were in that pantry."

"Oh!" I gave him a little shove that would have been playful if we'd been in the school hall. But here, alone in the sauna, it was my hand on his hard bare chest. I swallowed and tried to pretend I shoved half-naked boys in the sauna every day of the week. "You guys have big mouths."

"Like Chloe didn't tell you every move Gavin tried to make on her while they watched basketball on TV at his house last night. Or *didn't* watch basketball."

He had me there.

"So, Gavin and Chloe are otherwise occupied," Nick mused. "Davis and Liz are in the hot tub. You and I are alone. We might as well make the best of it."

As if I weren't hot enough already, I felt the heat rising through me, burning every inch of my skin. I blushed so hard that my face burned at the thought that my fantasies for four years, and specifically my dreams since last Friday in the hall, were about to come true.

A small space had opened between us when I'd shoved him. Now he closed that space again. His long, muscular leg touched my leg inch for inch—stuck to it, in fact, in the shadowy wet room. His long fingers found my bare tummy again and splayed wide across it, with his hot palm centered on my belly button.

"I love saunas, don't you?" he purred, leaning close to my face. "The heat." A lock of his dark hair stuck to my wet cheek. "The steam."

My heart knocked so hard against my chest that I could hardly stand it. "The scent of eucalyptus," I suggested before I thought about whether this added to the romance of the situation. "Smells like a bottle of my granddaddy's Old Spice that's been fermenting in his attic since 1969." I cringed. I just couldn't leave it alone and enjoy the moment, could I?

Nick pressed his lips together to keep from laughing. He nodded sagely. "I'll never think about this scent quite the same way, that's for sure." But Nick had a one-track mind, and even my lame jokes couldn't distract him. One of his hands still moved on my tummy. The other picked up my hand and moved it to his thigh.

Talk about a body like a rock.

I wanted to do this—had wanted it forever—but somehow I had thought there would be more preamble to it, more than fifteen minutes of flirting in the school hall. Even though I'd admittedly accepted every advance he made on me, picking up my hand and putting it on his thigh seemed mighty forward of him. I didn't take the radical step of *removing* my hand, but I did open my mouth to act all indignant.

He put two fingers to my lips to stop me from talking. He knew me pretty well. His mouth close to my ear, he growled, "You know, you and I *are* exes."

"So?" I asked around his fingers. My skin tingled with excitement, or possibly eucalyptus poisoning.

He leaned so close, I could feel his breath on my cheek, cool compared with the hot air. "If we weren't exes," he whispered, "it might be different. But we are. We won't do anything we haven't done before. What could it hurt?" His dark eyes looked deep into mine

73

for a few more seconds. Slowly he peeled his fingers away from my lips like he was afraid of what would escape my mouth.

What came to mind: *Oooh, yes, please, thank you.* But I couldn't let him know how much I wanted this. Sarcasm, I needed some sarcasm. "What a bunch of bull," I breathed. "Haven't you learned *anything* since the seventh grade?"

"One way to find out," he purred, moving in. He slipped his hand around the back of my neck, and then—

invert

(in′ vərt) *n.* **1.** a handstand on the lip of the half-pipe course **2.** Hayden turning the tables on Nick

—I hesitated.

I *never* hesitated. Hesitating in the slalom could cost me the race. Hesitating in the half-pipe could earn me a concussion. Hesitating on a jump could get me killed— and since I did have a tendency to hesitate there, I did not go off jumps.

And I knew better than to hesitate with Nick. That would show weakness, and he would swoop in and take advantage of me. Better to keep him off guard if I could.

Yet here we were, inches away from each other in the hot shadowy sauna, breathing hard, looking into each other's eyes, with my hand on his chest to keep him from coming any closer. He glanced to my lips, then focused on my eyes again, genuinely perplexed. Like he wasn't Nick at all but that boy my age, someone without filthy rich parents, someone unsure and terrified of messing this up.

Someone like me. I was terrified of messing this up, too. Which was exactly why I held him off. I *wanted* to believe he was unsure and vulnerable like me. But those old suspicions about Nick resurfaced. I'd waited too long for this, and I wanted to make sure we were doing it right.

"What's up?" he prompted me, cluing me in that I'd guessed correctly about him. Not a gentle *What's the matter, dear Hayden?* but a sharp *What's up?* like a boy growing impatient while bowling a girl over.

"Uh, I don't know," I stammered. "I just don't get a good vibe about this."

"You don't get a good *vibe*?" Although Nick controlled his emotions carefully, I could tell he was mad. This frightened me a little. I held the dubious honor of being the one person who could make cool, collected Nick lose his temper.

I wanted to be honest with him and give good reasons for balking, so I wouldn't hurt his feelings just in case he was being straight with me after all. I said slowly, "Well, for starters, from some of the things you said in the hall on Friday, I was thinking you might ask me to the Poser concert, but you haven't said another word about it."

I watched him closely as I said this. He watched me too, his dark eyes giving away nothing but anger.

I swallowed. "You've said Chloe invited you here for my victory party. I saw you out on your deck during the competition, so I know you remembered it was going on. But you haven't asked me anything about the contest, either."

His lips parted. I watched his soft lips (at least, I remembered them from seventh grade as soft) and waited for him to explain himself. But after a moment he closed his mouth again, and his dark eyes glinted harder.

I had desperately wanted to be wrong about Nick. I had wished he honestly liked me. But his silence and his anger were convincing me otherwise. That made *me* angry. And when I got angry, I was anything but silent.

"You've pretty much ignored me for the past four years, except to insult me or to throw something at me. Then suddenly you want to make out just when our friends get together? You don't act like you're very fond of me. You act like I'm convenient. You would have made out with any chick you happened upon in the sauna, from the hotel maid to the lady in room 3B. I'm not sure I *do* want to end our trial separation. We have irreconcilable differences." By the time I got all of this out, I was shouting at him. I'd known I was angry at him, but I hadn't realized I'd been storing up *that* much resentment for four years.

Apparently, neither had he. His hand suddenly tensed on my tummy, and I suppressed the urge to say *oof*. Nick and I had been pressing into each other on the bench, our thighs touching. Our heads were coming closer together with every word we uttered. If someone had interrupted us just then (which they wouldn't, because we would hear the hall door squeak first), they would think we were about to kiss. They would never understand how much tension rode on every word as Nick looked into my eyes and the following words slid out of his mouth and straight into my heart like slivers of glass: "You have a lot of freaking nerve." He sat back against the wooden wall, sliding his hand off my tummy and his thigh out from under my hand (nooooo!).

Clearly I couldn't read Nick as well as I'd thought. I hadn't wanted to make him angry if he really did care about me. I'd only wanted him to get his hands off me if I didn't mean anything to him. Now that it appeared I *did* mean something, and I'd hurt his feelings, my goal now was to get his hands back *on* me. "I'm not trying to make you mad," I said quickly. "I'm not even saying I'm right. This just seems very sudden, and I wanted to talk about it with you a little mo—"

"Forget it, Hayden." His skin glowed with sweat in the low light of the sauna, and his dark hair stuck to his forehead in wet black wisps. He breathed hard like the football team had just given him a good workout. Or like *I* had. And he looked like I'd slapped him.

But even without the hurt expression on

his handsome face, I would have known I'd seriously wounded him because he called me *Hayden* instead of *Hoyden*. Like my mother using my full name, Hayden Christine O'Malley, it meant I was in big trouble.

He went on, "I can't believe you would say something like that to me." He folded his big arms on his bare chest. "I mean, even if you don't care about *me*, I can't believe you would be that much of a bitch to *anyone*. That's just cruel."

The thing to do then was to make a snappy comeback and stomp out of the sauna, never to return. I got called the B-word a lot, undeservedly in my opinion, just because I had red hair and I said what I thought, perhaps a tad too loudly.

But all I could do was sit there on the bench, staring at Nick with my mouth open and tears in my eyes. I couldn't get over the feeling of seeing him for the first time tonight as younger and vulnerable, more like me. It hurt that I had hurt him. It hurt more that he had hurt me back.

Outside the sauna, the hall door squealed open. Someone was coming.

"Great," I breathed. Chloe had invited Nick over here tonight because he'd held my hand in the hall and she'd thought there was more to come. Even once I explained to Chloe that we officially hated each other now and that nothing had happened between us, Nick and I would not live down getting caught together in the sauna. All my friends would tease me about Nick even more, and I would *never* be able to get him off my mind.

Strangely, Nick didn't seem the least bit concerned about Gavin catching us and teasing us in class forevermore. He still stared at me like I'd slapped him. Okay, I'd slapped him a lot in class over the years, when he had shot spitballs at me or tried to write his name on my arm. This time he stared at me like I'd slapped him when he didn't deserve it.

The sauna door swung open. "*There* you are," Chloe exclaimed at me with her fists on her hips. Her eyes slid to Nick.

Gavin appeared over her shoulder. "And there *you* are," he called to Nick. His eyes slid to me.

Liz and Davis crowded the doorway, too. All four of them now wore bathing suits, which meant they'd intended to join us in the sauna. Suddenly it was way too hot and I couldn't breathe.

"God, it's like a *sauna* in here," I muttered at the same time Nick mumbled, "I was just leaving. This place is full of hot air." Too late I realized we were pushing through our friends in the doorway at the same time. We couldn't have acted more guilty.

I reached the hallway free and clear. Someone big padded behind me—Nick, I assumed—but I didn't look back. I burst through the squealing door, slipped into the women's locker room, and rushed under a cold shower with my bikini still on. "Eek!" Maybe if I stood there long enough, the lingering lust I felt for Nick would wash away, along with the regret that we hadn't kissed in the sauna.

The cold water bouncing off my skull only gave me a headache. I'd rejected Nick, yes. But the more I thought about it, the more his reaction seemed completely uncalled-for. I'd been called the B-word before, but never by Nick.

I turned off the water and pushed through the door on the opposite side of the locker room, into the cold night. I dashed for the heated pool, jumping in without looking first to see who I'd be sharing it with. Of course, Nick sat alone on the submerged stairs with his elbows behind him on the wall, watching me as I came up for air. Everyone else must be inside.

He didn't take the opportunity to leap across the pool and push me under, as he usually would have. He just stared me down, frowning, and flicked his wet hair out of his eyes with his pinkie. When I was little I'd spent a lot of time at the Tennessee Aquarium in Chattanooga. Now it was like Nick and I were separated by one of those foot-thick walls of specially tempered glass. We could see each other. We could even long for each other. But even if we both had put our hands up to the glass, we could never have touched. The glass between us was smooth and cold.

"Congratulations to you," the voices of the others sang from behind the slowly moving door. Gavin held it open for Chloe, who paraded out with the cake, and Liz, who carried paper plates and forks and napkins. As soon as everyone was clear of the door, Gavin and Davis made a run for the pool and jumped in to avoid the frigid air just like I had, but the girls sang on. "Congratulations, dear Hayden, congratulations to you!"

Liz's dark hair had kinked into tight

curls from the hot tub, and Chloe had carefully pinned up her long blond hair to keep it from getting wet in the pool. Chloe and Liz looked so adorable in their own ways, and so happy to be celebrating my victory, that I remembered for the first time in an hour this night was for *me*, not them, and definitely not Nick. I should enjoy it. Like Josh had warned me, my little baby snowboarding career might end in a stupendous crash when I took my first lesson with Daisy Delaney and she discovered I was afraid of heights. This night was all I knew I had.

"Thank y'all so much," I said, meaning it. I ignored Gavin echoing *y'all*, making fun of my Tennessee accent. I also ignored the fact that Nick was *not* echoing *y'all* like he usually would.

"You're-hur-hur welcome," Chloe said, teeth chattering as she set down the cake at the edge of the pool. Liz set down the plates, too. They waded into the pool, cut the cake from there, and passed around big slices. White cake with white icing, a pure sugar rush—not something I normally would have included in my health-conscious diet, but exactly what I needed when, frankly, this strange episode with Nick had gotten me down.

Liz handed me a plate, careful not to drip pool water on it. I was just taking my first bite when Nick spoke to me in a voice so kind, I knew something ugly was coming. "So, Hayden. What was your time on the slalom?"

"A minute seventeen," I told him, stuffing the next bite of cake into my mouth while watching him warily.

"That's funny," he said between bites. "Didn't you come in first in the girls' division? Because that's three seconds slower than the third-place time for the boys' division in your age group."

Everyone in the pool looked at me. They expected a rebuttal.

For once, I didn't have one.

Chloe extended her hand toward Nick. "Give me back that cake."

He held it away from her. "No, it's good."

"Give it. I don't like where you're going with this."

"No, I'm hungry." Wisely, he waded into the deeper end of the pool, where Chloe would not follow him if she wanted to keep her hair dry. Holding his cake and fork at chest-level above the surface of the water, he looked straight at me and said, "I just think that unless you compete with everyone, it's not really a competition." His dark eyes dropped to his plate, and he shoveled a big bite of cake into his mouth. He had basically told me my win today didn't matter, *and* I was not quite as important as cake.

I opened my mouth to holler at him. I was so angry, I had no idea what I would have said.

Luckily all I got out was a noise like *nyah* before Chloe interrupted me. "That's ridiculous. Girls and boys compete separately in almost every sport. You don't have girls on your football team."

"That's because girls would suck," Gavin offered. Nick waded back across the pool so they could bump fists. As he passed, the movement of his big body splashed water on my cake.

I slid my plate onto the pool deck and opened my mouth to lay into Nick with the insult he deserved.

But all I got out was something that sounded like *yerg* before Liz talked over me.

"Basic physics. The average boy is bigger than the average girl. Girls don't play football with boys because they'd get crushed. Girls have slower times than boys in the slalom because they're not as heavy. You should have seen Hayden's 900 in the half-pipe. Not a single boy did a 900 today, not even the guy who came in first in the oldest boys' division."

"That's because he's not that good," Nick countered. "Even *I* could beat that guy."

"Besides," Davis spoke up, "this was a local competition. You never know who'll show up for those. It would be different if she stepped up to a higher level. The men's Olympics are an event. The women's Olympics are a bathroom break."

"They are not!" I gasped, instinctively coming to the defense of snowboarding chicks, my idols. *Et tu, Brute?* I thought. This was getting ugly if even Davis, usually such a gentleman, was making light of my win.

Liz must have been thinking the same thing. After her big logical speech, she just gaped at him like she couldn't believe he'd said this.

Chloe was the one who shouted, "The

three of you really mean Hayden didn't accomplish anything today? You weren't even there to watch her!"

Nick was, I thought. He was there on his deck. He'd made note of the slalom times. Now he cut his eyes at me, letting me know this had flashed through his mind, too.

"We didn't have to see her," he said. "Any snowboarder knows this about the sport. Women aren't anything compared with men. Hayden won lessons with Daisy Delaney, right? Pit Daisy Delaney against Shaun White. He'd crush her. Hell, pit Daisy Delaney against Mason Aguirre."

"Yeah!" Gavin took up the challenge. "Did you see the X Games on TV a couple of weeks ago? The guys stick 1260s on the slopestyle. They throw down back-to-back 1080s in the half-pipe or it's not even considered a run. The girls are lucky if they land a 900." He then created a range of Daisy Delaney slap-downs with every famous male snowboarder he could think of. Davis laughed, and he quietly offered suggestions when Gavin ran out of ideas. Chloe kept breaking in with protests, and Liz kept saying, "But . . ." From their separate places around the pool, all four of them waded closer as the talk got more heated, until they surrounded Nick and me on all sides.

But I didn't really hear them anymore. I stared at Nick in front of me. He stared back. We'd set this argument in motion, and now it kept rolling without us. No one seemed to notice we'd dropped out. I watched him, hoping I'd get some sign he was just kidding.

He watched me, too. But he never winked or made any move to break the tension. Everything he'd said about girls versus boys, he'd meant.

"So, you think you could have beaten the first-place guy?" I asked Nick.

He knew I'd said something. But he was listening to Gavin, and he couldn't hear me over the guffaws. With a last dark look at me, he turned toward the other boys and laughed.

I was angry now, truly angry. I'd worked hard to win that competition, and it *did* mean something. I slogged through the warm water and cold air, stopping right in front of him, my tummy only inches from his knees where he sat on the stairs. I said again, "Nick, you really think you could have beaten the first-place guy today if you'd only bothered to enter the competition?"

"Absolutely," he told me, still not looking or sounding like himself. He made cocky statements all the time, accepting challenges and taking bets. But his voice always held an ironic tone, like he was half-kidding and didn't believe it himself. This time he sounded like he believed it.

Or maybe the difference was in me, not him. Maybe after four years, I'd finally fallen out of love with him.

"Let's do it, then." I reached forward and poked his bare chest with two fingers like we were actors in a gangster movie. "You and me, on the slopes, head-to-head, the slalom and the half-pipe. I will kick." *Poke.* "Your." *Poke.* "Ass."

"Oooooh," the boys said. The moaning was so loud that I could have sworn Chloe and even Liz chimed in.

But all I saw was Nick in front of me, not budging a millimeter as I poked him, eyes frowning and lips curled in a tight smile. Quietly he told me, "Remember, you asked for it."

I did *not* ask for this attack. But I didn't dare defend myself or even hint at what had transpired between us in the sauna. The madder I got, the more he'd know I cared that he'd called me a bitch, and the worse I would hurt.

"Want to make it interesting?" Gavin asked, wading over. "Let's do this thing on Saturday. After Nick wins, the girls treat the guys to the Poser concert that night."

"You mean when Hayden wins, the boys treat the girls," Chloe corrected him. "That sounds fair."

"It's *not* fair," Davis protested. "After Nick wins, you'll just say conditions were different when Hayden came down, and that's what made her slower. Like, it started snowing."

"Or it *stopped* snowing," Gavin said.

"Or the wind was harder," Davis said.

"Or the wind was *softer*," Gavin said. "Girls will whine about anything."

"Fine!" Liz broke in, obviously agitated. She never spoke this loudly, much less broke in. "Instead of a slalom where they come down one at a time, they'll come down together, like in a boardercross."

"It's still not fair," Gavin pointed out. "No matter how high Nick goes in the half-pipe, you'll say, 'But Hayden landed a 900!'" He ended in a high-pitched voice that none of us girls had used since the second grade.

"Leave it to me," Chloe said ominously. "I'll find three impartial judges. Even *you* won't be able to complain." She used one finger on her right hand to pretend to scribble a note to herself on the palm of her left hand. Then she put her hands down and glared around the pool. "In the meantime, we've had just about enough of you guys and your sexist attitudes. Find your own way out. Come on, ladies." She picked up the cake, and Liz obediently gathered the plates.

I still crouched in the warm pool in front of Nick, stunned. Whether the girls treated the boys to Poser tickets or the boys treated the girls, we'd be paired off: Liz with Davis, Chloe with Gavin. Did this mean Nick and I had . . . a date?

That was *so* not going to happen.

Dazed, I moved past him up the stairs, following Chloe. Nick caught me by the wrist. Our hands were wet and I could have slipped out of his grasp, but I didn't. I stopped beside him on the stairs, shivering in the cold air, waiting breathlessly for him to break the date Chloe and Gavin had arranged for us, or to make a snide comment about it.

"We need a tiebreaker," he said, loudly enough for everyone to hear, but looking only at me. "Not that I'm saying I won't win the boardercross *and* the half-pipe. But I want to make sure I win fair and square. Just in case, we need to add a third event. Like a big air."

"Done," Chloe said quickly. "We'll bury you. Come on, Hayden."

Funny, I must have been riding waves of adrenaline the whole afternoon and night. I'd exerted myself on the slopes in the competition, but I hadn't felt the least bit sore. Now I suddenly felt it. My muscles were sore and tired, my eyes strained, and my brain hurt just thinking about the jump at the slopes, the one stunt I hadn't tried and didn't plan to. But Nick was right. This whole argument was about who was the better boarder overall. How could I be better than him if I couldn't go off a jump, one of the biggest parts of this sport?

"Good idea," I heard Gavin say as I sloshed out of the pool.

"No problemo," Davis said knowingly. The *smack* of their high five echoed against the wall of the hotel.

Before I closed the hotel door behind

me, I stole one more glance back at Nick. Maybe he hadn't meant to set me up to fail. Maybe he'd momentarily forgotten I was afraid of heights. But no, he turned around on the steps and looked straight at me, still wearing that small smile. He flicked his wet hair out of his eyes with his pinkie, as if to show me yet again how little he thought of me. He knew exactly what he'd done.

comp

(kämp) *n.* **1.** a snowboarding contest **2.** Hayden vs. Nick

Heart racing and mind whirling, I walked into the locker room and changed into my clothes, hardly hearing Chloe and Liz's discussion echoing against the tile walls about what pigs boys could be. I was calculating how to fix this terrible situation. Maybe I could do the jump this time, and then I wouldn't have to worry about Daisy Delaney challenging me in the back bowls. Maybe all I'd ever needed to get over my fear of heights was the tall, dark, and hunky heir to a meat fortune to insult me and make fun of me. But gosh, it sure would be easier if I could *talk* my way out of this whole contest. "What?" I said.

Liz was standing in front of me. She looked a bit frazzled with her damp curls in her face. Obviously she'd been trying to get my attention for a while. "I *said*, have you seen your butt?"

"Is that a rhetorical question?" I craned my neck to take a gander at my backside.

Chloe clarified, "She means you have 'boy toy' written across the back of your jeans."

"Oh." I nodded. "They're Josh's."

"You say that as if it explains everything." Liz cocked her head to one side and considered me while buttoning her cardigan. "My stepbrothers don't write 'boy toy' across the back of their jeans. They only say the entire alphabet while burping."

"That's nothing. Josh can recite the Gettysburg Address. Listen, y'all." I pulled my hair free from the collar of my sweater. The long strands were damp, reminding me I'd just been in the pool with Nick. I could *still* be in the pool with Nick if he weren't such an ass. "I want to call off this contest."

Chloe's eyes narrowed. "Don't you dare."

Liz's eyes got big as she wailed, "Hayden, you can't!"

"I want to call it off." I took a deep breath before I warned them, "Otherwise, plan to buy Poser tickets for the boys. There's no way I'll win."

"Of course you'll win!" Chloe exclaimed. "You'll probably beat Nick in that race thing—"

"Boardercross," I corrected her. Chloe owned a snowboard, and that's about as far as her knowledge of the sport went.

"—and you'll blow him away in the trick part."

"Half-pipe. And then there's the jump."

They both just stared at me with their arms folded. They'd been pushing me to get over my fear of heights and go pro, so this was no way to argue myself out of my new corner.

I started over. "Okay, here's the real deal. I regret what I lost with Everett Walsh—"

"Come off it," Chloe said. "Tell us another."

I swallowed. "—and I want to make sure y'all aren't making a huge mistake. I mean, I'm mad, too, but I'm always mad at Nick. Maybe you're blowing this out of proportion with Gavin and Davis. I know both of you looked forward to seeing them tonight. Your evening with them got off to an excellent start. And now you're sending them home early, all because of this stupid challenge? I wish I'd never said anything." At least *that* part was the truth.

"Gavin told me a dumb-blonde joke last week when he made a ninety-eight on the chemistry test and I made a ninety-seven," Chloe said.

"That's just Gavin." I couldn't believe I was defending that jerk, but I really did think Chloe was overreacting. "Gavin would make fun of you for a hair out of place. He's just feeling around for material."

"He can't feel *there*," she said vehemently. "He can make jokes, and I'll giggle and pretend he's actually funny, up to a point. But if he tries to tell me I'm less of a person because I'm a girl? Or *you* are? That's where I draw the line." She pulled her bag from a locker and slammed the metal door.

"But you can't blame Davis," I reasoned, turning to Liz. "He didn't start it."

"He didn't stop it," Liz said, not looking up from tying her boots. "He was so disrespectful of you on your big day."

"But he didn't mean anything by it," I pointed out, "unlike Gavin, and definitely unlike Nick. Davis is naturally a sweet-natured person. He's just been hanging around Nick and Gavin too long. It's a wonder they don't have him stealing candy from babies, or blasting rap music out of his car stereo in front of the retirement home."

Liz stood, shaking her head. For a moment I hoped some water had dripped down her face from her damp curls—but no. She had tears in her eyes. "My boyfriend can't treat my friends that way."

"Oh God!" I exclaimed, really desperate now. "Look at me." I stood in front of both of them. To Liz I said, "You and Davis are adorable together." I moved to Chloe. "And you and Gavin are—"

She raised her eyebrows at me.

"—*interesting* together. You can't let my fight with Nick ruin your relationships with your hot boyfriends. Come on, now. My fight with Nick has been going on for years. It's like this black hole, with gravity so strong that not even light can escape, sucking in winter breaks and dates and whole relationships, until the world—are you listening to me?" When I'd started waxing poetic,

Chloe's attention had wandered around the room. I grabbed her chin and turned her face to me again. "Until the very world is devoid of love!"

"It's not *that* bad," Nick's voice came faintly through the locker room wall.

We all looked at one another.

"Let's go up to my apartment," Chloe said. "Forget them. I have something in my room that will cheer us up, and it's *much* better than boys."

Chloe was serious about putting the boys in Time Out for the time being, and Liz seemed serious, too. Now that I knew Nick was in the locker room next door, I listened for him and wondered whether the boys would eventually follow us to Chloe's family's apartment at the back of the building, overlooking the ski slopes. Chloe and Liz clomped up the stairs like they weren't giving the boys a second thought.

I slowed on the steps. Chloe and Liz reached the top of the staircase and pushed into the hall above me, leaving the door to close slowly and bump shut behind them. I was alone. I turned around and watched the door at the bottom of the staircase, waiting for Nick to appear. Wishing he would materialize so I could yell at him and get this weight off my chest.

I'd been so in love with him for that magical month in seventh grade, and so devastated to find out I was a joke to him. He must have sensed that I still liked him more than I was letting on, and now he was acting mean about it. *Why?* What had I ever done to him? I wanted to be furious with him about the girl snowboarder comments, the jump challenge, *everything*, but it just didn't make any sense.

I stood there so long, staring a hole in the closed door at the bottom of the stairs, willing it to open and Nick to walk in and explain himself to me, that I got dizzy in the long white room. The dread of snowboarding off that jump came back to me in a rush. I clung to the railing to keep from falling down the stairs.

"Hayden," Liz called from the hall.

"Coming!" I shook my head to clear it, then ran up the stairs to my friends without looking back again.

In Chloe's bedroom, she and Liz sat on Chloe's fluffy pink king-size bed, waiting expectantly. Uh-oh. Sure enough, the second I closed the door behind me, they both squealed, "Did you and Nick make out?"

I sighed. "For a second there, I thought we were going to."

"But you didn't?" Chloe wailed.

I flopped onto the foot of the bed and stretched out on my back. "No. We had an argument, and he called me a bitch."

"What!" Liz exclaimed. "That's so disrespectful!"

"That doesn't sound like Nick," Chloe said. "What exactly led up to this?"

Thinking back, I sat up with an enormous groan. The whole evening had been so confusing and frustrating and *mortifying*. Not like the seventh grade, but close. "I walked in on him in the sauna. We joked around. You know how we do."

Liz and Chloe nodded. Chloe motioned for me to hurry up with my story.

"I thought he was going to kiss me, and I stopped him." I put up a hand to Chloe's chest just as I had to Nick's. Then, when I realized what I was doing, I hastily jerked my hand away. "Sorry. Didn't mean to feel you up."

"It's quite all right," Chloe said.

"Why did you stop him?" Liz shrieked impatiently.

I rubbed my temple. My headache from

the cold shower hadn't quite dissipated. "I don't know. It seemed like that was all he wanted, and I couldn't let him take advantage of me."

"Maybe he thought that's all *you* wanted from *him*," Chloe suggested.

I frowned at this disturbing possibility. "Maybe. It's hard to have a heart-to-heart with someone who throws stuff at you and calls you a fire-crotch and a bitch."

"Is that all that happened?" Liz prompted me. "You stopped him from kissing you, and he called you a bitch?"

"No," I admitted. "I told him I didn't want to kiss him because he hadn't asked me to the Poser concert. He hadn't asked me about winning the competition. He acted like I was just a convenient catch because all of y'all are dating. I told him we had irreconcilable differences."

Chloe gasped. "Like in a divorce? Hayden, why did you say that?"

I supposed it *did* sound ugly, now that I thought about it. But not *that* ugly. "We were both making divorce jokes in the hall last Friday. He started it."

"Hayden." Liz leaned forward and took me by both shoulders, bracing me for the bad news she was about to break. "Nick's mother left his father on Sunday."

"What!" I hollered, jumping off the bed to pace the floor.

"He told Gavin and Davis," Chloe said, "and they told Liz and me. Nick must have thought you knew. If *I* were him, and you blew me off and made divorce jokes, I guess I would have called you a bitch, too."

I stopped pacing and put my hands in my hair to keep from throttling her. "Jesus, Chloe! Why did you invite him over here in the middle of his family troubles?"

"He's friends with Gavin and Davis," she said. "He needed to get out of the house and forget about it for a night. He needs all our support right now."

Guilt trip.

"And you didn't have a date tonight because you broke up with Everett," Chloe said.

I took my hands out of my hair so I wouldn't tear it out. "Everett and his mama broke up with *me*, thank you very much."

"You shouldn't have made out with him in his mother's scrapbooking room," Liz said sagely.

"We're seventeen," I snapped, "and Everett

and I had been dating for two months when that happened. What were we supposed to do, eat dinner with his family and keep our hands on the table where everyone could see them? I mean, you and Davis are Mr. and Mrs. Polite Reserve, and even you were macking in the hot tub an hour ago." I picked up a pink fuzzy pillow that had fallen from the bed and threw it at Liz.

"You *were?*" Chloe gushed. "You *what?* Hello, I need the details of Liz and Davis."

"Hayden!" Liz squealed, ducking behind Chloe. "I'm not saying you shouldn't have made out with Everett. I'm saying you shouldn't have done it in his mother's scrap-booking room. Location, location, location. You might have disorganized her supplies. Some people are very particular about their chipboard getting mixed up with their card-stock."

I closed my eyes, inhaled through my nose, and felt my lungs fill with air. My blood spread the life-giving oxygen through-out my body.

"Watch out," Chloe whispered to Liz. "She's doing yoga."

My eyes snapped open. So much for con-trolling my temper. "Why the hell didn't you tell me Nick's mother left before I went into the sauna with him?" I hollered at Chloe.

"We didn't know he was here!" Liz came to Chloe's defense.

"And if we'd warned you about him *before* he got here," Chloe explained, "you would have known he was coming. We didn't want you to leave. The two of you are surprisingly hard to throw together, let me tell you."

"I'm not buying it," I informed Chloe. "You were distracted. You had your mind on taking inventory."

Liz giggled, turned red, and fell back on the pillows.

"Taking inventory requires enormous concentration!" Chloe said with a straight face, but she was blushing, too.

I was glad for them, really. I was happy they'd had fun with their boyfriends, at least for a little while, and I hoped they didn't push this bet too far.

At the same time, I was very angry with them for contributing to this terrible mix-up with Nick. As supportive as Chloe and Liz usually were to me, I couldn't help thinking at that moment that I had Very Bad Friends.

Liz sat up again and wiped her eyes. "Do you want me to tell Davis to tell Nick that you didn't know anything about his parents when you were in the sauna with him?"

I shook my head no. "It sounds too much like a debauched game of Telephone. This whole thing seems very seventh grade. Besides, it's actually good this happened. Nick is a smooth talker. It took him getting furious for me to find out how he really feels about me. I don't want or need a boyfriend who thinks so little of my snowboarding skills and questions the very relevance of women's athletics. I'll admit, I may have carried a torch for him all these years. He just blew it out. So consult me the next time you want to play Cupid for me. And don't choose me a boy with four or five girls in a holding pattern. Nick Krieger is all wrong for me. Stop throwing us together."

Chloe and Liz stared at me from the bed.

"Okay?" I prompted them.

"Okay," they agreed, way too agreeably.

Even after tonight's disaster, I got the feeling they were not through with Nick and me yet.

"I'm glad this happened, too," Liz said quickly. "It'll give you the push you need to get over your fear of heights."

"Yeah, about that bet." I rubbed my temple again, massaging away the headache that throbbed harder than ever. "I'm sorry, y'all, but there's no way I'm going off that jump. I'll buy the Poser tickets for you." I had been saving for another snowboard—they didn't last forever, the way I abused the half-pipe—but fair was fair.

"Oh," Liz cried sympathetically, "you don't have to do—"

"You will not lose this bet!" Chloe insisted. "We are showing up those boys, and you are going off that jump. I'll board with you tomorrow and coach you."

Now *there* was some motivation to get over this problem quickly. Chloe was a notorious betty. On the rare occasion when she graced the slopes with her presence, boys zoomed toward her because she was so cute in her pink snowsuit, then zoomed away again as she lost control and threatened to crash into them. She'd made the local snowboarding news a few years ago when she lost control at the bottom of the main run, boarded right through the open door of the ski lodge, skidded to a stop at the entrance to the café, and asked for a table for one.

"I'm working at the city library tomorrow," Liz said, "but I'll ski with you and coach you on Thursday."

"Have you actually tried to go off the jump and failed," Chloe asked me, "or do you not even try?"

"I don't even try." I didn't like to look at the thing. I averted my eyes when Josh and his friends jumped off.

"So, now you'll try," she decreed. "What's the worst that could happen?"

I opened my mouth to describe the worst that could happen. I could freeze up ten yards from the precipice, and all four spots where my leg had been broken would throb deep inside, even though I'd been healed for years. I would relive my rappelling accident. A series of sickening jerks as every safety belt and harness failed, one by one, and let me fall.

"Hayden, what's the matter?" Liz called. "You look like you saw a ghost."

I looked at her and then at Chloe, biting

my lip to keep from crying. I didn't want to let them down, but this was a lot of pressure for what was supposed to be a carefree winter break.

Chloe clapped her hands, snapping me out of it. "I almost forgot what I found to show you! It's so good, it'll make this whole night worthwhile."

The three of us settled on her bed and ate CONGRATULATIONS HAYDEN! cake straight out of the box with our forks while she passed around this secret treasure that was better than boys (as if). She'd been cleaning out her closet—some people *did* clean out their closets, I supposed—when she'd come across a teen fashion mag–style quiz with twenty questions that she'd written and all three of us had answered back in seventh grade. Our handwriting was young and loopy. We'd dotted the *i*'s with stars and flowers and hearts.

1. If you accidentally got locked inside the school for an entire weekend with a blizzard coming, and the only way you could survive was to share body heat with the boy trapped inside with you, who would you want it to be?

Hayden: Barry Yates

Chloe: Ollie Cattrall

"Ollie Cattrall," Chloe mused. "Right after we wrote this, he moved to Massachusetts. I should look him up on Facebook."

"Chloe!" Liz exclaimed, horrified.

"And then he would post a comment on *my* page," Chloe explained, "and Gavin would see it. This would show Gavin he's not the only man interested in me, and he might treat me a little nicer."

"Or," I pointed out, "this would show him that Ollie Cattrall, who lives two thousand miles away, either is being polite to you or is hitting on you because he cannot get a date at his own school. Which makes one wonder if he had to take his Facebook picture carefully in very low lighting."

She glared at me. "Moving on."

Liz: Davis Goggins

"Awww," Chloe and I both said. I reached out to pinch Liz's cheek. She and Davis hadn't been dating long, but it was so sweet she'd thought about him that way back in seventh grade. Almost as if they were destined to be together.

"I'm not sure anymore," Liz grumbled. "Ask me again after he pays for my Poser ticket."

2. If you were suddenly transported to the 1800s and you had to marry a boy in our class to be saved from an arranged marriage with an evil viscount,

(Chloe read a lot of historical romances.)

who would you want to marry?

Hayden: Mark Jones
Chloe: Scotty Yarbrough
Liz: Everett Walsh

"Everett Walsh!" Chloe exclaimed. I fell off the bed laughing.

Liz folded her arms and tried to scowl at us, but I could tell she was having a hard time keeping a straight face. "What's wrong with Everett Walsh?" she sputtered. "I didn't know when we wrote this in seventh grade that Hayden would hook up with him later. I saw him first."

"He's so straitlaced," Chloe said. "Not exactly the ideal hero of a romance."

"Watch out for his mama," I advised Liz.

"I was answering the question you asked," Liz told Chloe self-righteously. "If your family threatened you with an arranged marriage in the 1800s, you'd want someone on your side who was very mature and organized, who could approach the situation logically and help you out of it. In the 1800s, Everett Walsh would have been a barrister. He'd be perfect for the job."

"I'd rather have the evil viscount," I said.

We stayed late at Chloe's, giggling over the other eighteen questions. The night was so fun, and I loved reliving these memories with Liz and Chloe. I hoped we stayed friends forever and would someday look back fondly on *this* night, just as we were looking back on *that* night four years ago. And I hoped we wouldn't remember this as the night we foolishly cut those cute boys loose.

Because although the night was fun, this quiz definitely was *not* better than boys. I didn't admit it to Liz and Chloe, but I remembered exactly what I'd been thinking when I took this quiz in seventh grade.

I'd been hoping I wouldn't go to hell for the little white lies I was telling. I would have been mortified to say so, but when I'd picked Barry Yates or Mark Jones or any boy for the rest of the quiz, I'd always meant Nick.

"Hayden Christine O'Malley!"

I started awake. White morning sunlight reflected off the snow outside and bounced through my bedroom window. My body still felt sore and my mind was wiped out from the contest and the argument with Nick yesterday. For my dad to be hollering at me like that, I must have been so tired when I came in last night that I left dishes on the kitchen counter instead of putting them in the dishwasher, or—worse—I forgot to let Doofus out. That really *would* be a mess to clean up.

I reached out from under the covers, opened my bedroom door, and called down the stairs, "Yes, honored father?"

"Get down here."

I jumped out of bed, eager to please. That was the only way I knew how to take the edge off the punishment he chose to hand down. Luckily, I glanced in the mirror, because I'd slept in a Burton Snowboards T-shirt. This would not help me look innocent at *all*. I pulled that off and pawed through my dresser for something more ladylike and less . . . dangerous. Hello Kitty!

I galloped downstairs—tripped over Doofus at the foot of the staircase—and slipped into my chair at the kitchen table. A plate of whole wheat pancakes and tofu bacon was waiting for me. I hoped the steam and the giant innocent face of a kitten on my T-shirt would blunt whatever blow was coming.

My dad had his back to me at the stove. Mom had already left to open the health club. Across the table from me, Josh put his fork down and made a small twisting motion with his fingers. I wasn't sure, but he seemed to be telling me I was screwed.

Dad set his own plate at the table and sat down. He drew out the torture, taking a bite, chewing slowly, staring a hole through me without speaking.

Finally I said, "Good morning, respected padre."

"Hmph," he said. "Your brother tells me that by giving in to your acrophobia, thereby ruining your chances of a professional snowboarding career, you are also sabotaging *his* chances of having the same sort of career through no special effort on his part. Shame on you! You're grounded."

I sniffed. "Did you really wake me up early during my winter break just so you could make a sarcastic comment to Josh?"

Josh stuck out his tongue at me, then took a huge bite of pancake.

Dad pointed at me with his fork. "Yes, sorry. If I'd waited until you woke up on your own to make that sarcastic comment, I might have been late for work."

I yawned.

"But while we're on the subject, Josh is right. His motivation is self-serving, but he's right about your phobia. If you really want a pro boarding career, sounds to me like you'd better get over your fear or throw away your chance to impress Daisy Delaney. No pressure."

I grumbled, "You have no idea."

Though my stomach hurt, somehow I swallowed breakfast. Thirty minutes later, Josh and I pulled on our layers of boarding clothes—tripped over Doofus—and headed outside for the bus. But when I opened the mud room door and looked down at the doormat, I stopped short. Josh ran smack into me and nearly brought us both down. *"Forward,"* he said. "Most people walk *forward*. What is it?"

I picked up the local newspaper and held it out to him, speechless for once. It was rolled, but on the part we could see, a huge headline proclaimed, SNOWBOARDING COMPETITION . . . And a huge photo showed me in midair, snowboard and parka and red hair bright against the blue sky.

Then I pulled the newspaper back from Josh and took another look. "I've never seen myself snowboard before. Check my excellent form! I would be ecstatic, except that my life is crumbling around me and stuff."

"Your life isn't crumbling around you. Just go off the damn jump." Josh grabbed the paper from me and slid off the rubber band. Unrolled, the news was even worse. The whole headline was SNOWBOARDING COMPETITION SHOWCASES LOCAL TALENT, and the caption under the photo read SNOWFALL HIGH SCHOOL JUNIOR HAYDEN O'MALLEY LANDS A FRONTSIDE 900 IN THE HALF-PIPE TO WIN THE GIRLS' 16 TO 18 DIVISION.

"Give me that, you little traitor." I grabbed the paper back. "I've got to hide this from Mom and Dad. You want them to make me spend my whole winter break in some shrink's office?"

"If it helps you get over your phobia, yeah. Anyway, if you hide the paper, Dad will just call the newspaper office to deliver another copy. And I don't know who you're calling little."

I knew one way to solve this argument. I carefully tore the whole article out of the front page, then rolled up the newspaper and slid the rubber band back on. "Doofus," I whispered. Poor Doofus, behind us in the mud room, stood up in a rush of jingling dog tags and slobber. I slipped the paper into his mouth and whispered, "Take this to Dad."

Doofus wagged his tail and trotted into the kitchen. We heard Dad say, "Did you bring me the paper? Good dog. Wait a minute. Bad dog!"

Josh softly closed the door behind us. "You've got to do something, Hayden. You just *can't* throw away this opportunity with Daisy."

"If it's a choice between that and me falling to my death, I sure as hell can!" I shrieked. As if in answer, ear-splitting brakes squealed downhill. "And now we're going to miss the bus!"

We waved our arms and skidded down the icy sidewalk with our snowboards as fast as we could. The bus driver was used to us and waited. Hardly anybody rode the bus this early—only a couple of other die-hard locals on winter break. We called hi to them in the back and sat down up front.

I heaved a deep sigh. "You're not the only one gunning for me to go off the jump. Now I've got Liz and Chloe on my case." Briefly I recounted my ugly convo with Nick last night and explained our snowboarding challenge—leaving out that I'd supposedly made Nick feel worse about his parents' separation on purpose, which was actually an accident.

Josh was staring at me with his brows down, perplexed. "Nick Krieger, of Krieger Meats and Meat Products?"

I nodded. "Yeah, *that* Nick Krieger."

"Why is Nick Krieger telling you that girl snowboarders are no good and your win doesn't mean anything? Does he like you or something? Make sure he knows we're vegetarian. Mom and Dad would die if they had to pay your dowry in kielbasa."

I gaped at Josh in disbelief. "What do you mean, does Nick like me? Is that how *you* flirt with girls you like? Tell them they're bad at stuff? Is that how you flirt with Gavin's sister?"

He blinked innocently. "Is that wrong?"

"I wouldn't say 'wrong.' I would say 'not the most efficient way of asking a girl to the middle school Christmas dance.'"

He wrinkled his nose and moved his mouth, imitating my scolding, so I knew I'd guessed correctly about the last time he'd bombed asking out Gavin's sister.

"Stop it." I slapped at him. "And tell me the truth. Do you agree with Nick that I'll never be as good as a boy, so there's no use trying?"

"Keep in mind that I have seen the answer key. I know what I'm supposed to say to stop you from hitting me."

"Uh-huh."

He leaned back against the salt-streaked window and considered me. "You are the most physically fit person I have ever met. I mean, I'm physically fit, too. I probably work out in the health club almost as much as you do. But I have been known to sneak a Pop-Tart out of the vending machine at school."

I gasped and put my hands to my mouth in mock horror.

"I know. It was whole grain, but still. You, on the other hand, are serious about keeping your body in top shape. You have a lot of natural athletic ability. And you got hurt all those years ago, which gives you extra drive like nobody else on the slopes."

I couldn't believe all this was coming out of Josh's mouth. Normally he was such a dork, but he did have his moments of depth. Right now he was looking me in the eye, letting me know he understood what a serious problem this was for me. I felt so much better just knowing that he cared.

"If you want to be a professional snowboarder," he went on, "the only thing holding you back is you. And I can help you there." He put his arm around me and squeezed way too hard on purpose. "Just leave it in the hands of me and my posse."

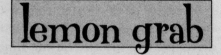

lemon grab

(leˈ mən grab) *n.* **1.** a trick in which the rider grabs both ends of the snowboard **2.** what Hayden feels like she's doing every time she talks to Nick

"AY-BATTA-BATTA-BATTA-BATTA-BATTA!" yelled Josh's fourteen-year-old friends. I ignored them and sped across the snow toward the jump.

"Schwing!" finished Josh. He made a batting motion with both arms.

I saw this out of the corner of my eye. I'd lost my focus on the end of the jump. There was no way I could go off the jump *now*. Hating the feeling of relief that washed through me, I slid to a stop next to the boys. I was careful to slice the bank with my snowboard, sending a wave of snow straight over them.

"Hey!" Josh protested. He shook snow off his hat. "I thought we were supposed to help you go off the jump. We were trying to distract you from your fear." He wiggled his gloved fingertips at me on *fear*.

"You're just giving her another excuse not to go off," Chloe said through her pink glove. She sat on a snowboarding trick rail nearby, chin in her hand, almost as frustrated with me as I was with myself.

In the boys' defense, they *had* stayed here with me for over an hour while Chloe coached me in getting over my fear of heights. I was asking a lot of all of them. I needed to end this *now*. Looking around at the blinding white slopes glittering in the bright sunshine, I tried to remember why this was so important. I needed to do this jump so I would believe in myself. To impress Daisy Delaney.

To show up Nick.

"Okay." I curled my arms up like a body-builder. "Cheer me on here."

"Yaaaaay." Chloe and the four boys

cheered and clapped with zero enthusiasm.

"I can do this," I insisted. "How many failed attempts is that?"

"Nine," Chloe said through her glove.

"There's no way I'm going to fail at this ten times in a row. I'm Hayden O'Malley! I won the Snowfall Amateur Challenge!"

"Wooooo," they moaned, no more excited than they'd been before.

"I shouldn't have to convince you to cheer for me." I reached down for a clod of snow and pelted Josh with it. Bull's-eye: It got him right on the goggles. "What happened to leaving it in the hands of you and your posse?"

He took off his goggles and wiped them on his snow pants. "That still seemed like a good idea, back on failed attempt number three."

"I'll show you," I grumbled. Anger was good for me when I tried something new with my board. Possibly Josh knew this and was acting like a butt on purpose. I tried not to think too much about that, or to remember how nice he'd been on the bus. I released my back boot from the binding and pushed myself along like I was riding a skateboard, up the hill and away from the edge of the jump. From here I could get a running start. Ideally, I would pick up enough speed that if I *did* chicken out at the last minute, it would be too late.

It was a gorgeous late morning with a cloudless, bright blue sky. No fog, no haze, so I could see all the way to the buildings of Snowfall at the bottom of the mountain, even pick out the festive red banners flying beneath the streetlamps.

That was a long way down.

I squeezed my eyes shut and inhaled through my nose. My blood spread the life-giving oxygen throughout my body.

I exhaled through my mouth and felt gravity pull the energy from my heart—

"No excuses this time!" Chloe's voice sounded hollow, like she was calling through her cupped hands.

—down through my legs, through my boots and snowboard, through the snow, to the rocks below. I was one with the mountain.

"Daisy Delaney would be halfway down the mountain by now," called Josh.

"Yeah!" came the voice of one of Josh's

friends. "You expect Daisy Delaney to wait for you to meditate every time you go off a cliff?"

So much for re-centering. Anger seemed to be a better motivator after all. I was a little angry at Chloe, plenty angry at Josh, and mega-angry at Nick for making me feel like a second-class snowboarder. Most of all, I was angry at myself for not being able to do this. I would show us all.

I burst into action, leaning down the hill to put all my weight into increasing my speed.

Snow arced away from me, and dark snowy trees flashed past. The jump came closer. I pictured how ecstatic I would feel when I finally made this happen. The jump loomed closer. I pictured myself going off the end.

I panicked. I skidded to a halt at the last second. Clumps of snow launched from the edge in slow motion and burst into smithereens on the snowpack below.

And then I realized I was still falling, following the momentum of my snowboard and slipping over the edge. I grabbed for anything, but there was nothing solid to grab. The jump was made of layers of packed snow. My slick waterproof mittens slipped on the edge. I banged my snowboard against the jump to free my feet from the bindings so I could get some traction with my boots, anything to keep from falling. Normally the catches were touchy, sometimes releasing at unfortunate times during the middle of a forceful trick—but now they wouldn't pop open, and my snowboard was a dead weight pulling me down. I was back in my wheelchair already.

No way! I would not break a leg again. I would not be an invalid. My arms ached from holding myself on the precipice. I was tiring myself out and doing myself no good. I inhaled through my nose and felt my lungs fill with air. My blood spread the life-giving oxygen throughout my body. I exhaled through my—

"Hayden!" Chloe screamed. "Stop doing yoga and climb your ass up the jump!" Her voice jogged like she was maneuvering toward me as fast as she could in her gear, falling in the snow.

I could hold on until she and the boys got to me. I slipped another inch, but that just sent another wave of adrenaline through my arms, helping me tighten my grip. I could hold on—

Strong hands circled both my wrists and pulled a little, then slid down to my upper arms and pulled harder. Thank God that Chloe had reached me in time. But now I was afraid I was too heavy for her and would pull her over with me. I looked up to tell her to let me go if she felt herself falling.

It was Nick. Goggles and snow half-covered his face. I recognized him by his jaw—which he set in a grimace as I watched. Maybe I was too heavy for *him*.

But then Chloe did arrive, leaning over the lip of the jump to grab one of my legs. Josh grabbed the end of my snowboard. Together they all hauled me up over the edge, then collapsed around me on the jump.

"Are you okay?" Chloe shrieked, kneeling over me. I nodded, panting, and patted her pink glove. She and Josh's friends plopped down with us in the snow.

"Y'all, thank you," I breathed. I lay on my back, staring up at the bright blue empty sky. Compared with the blue shadows below the lip of the jump, it was so bright and white up here. Thousands upon thousands of people must be skiing on the mountain today, but the snow muffled sound. All I heard was the seven of us struggling to get our breath back. Nick breathed closest to me, inhaling long and deep and exhaling big clouds of water vapor, like he was truly shaken by the idea of me falling and relieved he'd come to my rescue.

No, come on. He would have rescued anyone. He wouldn't let anybody fall off the end of the jump, even a stranger. In fact, he might not even recognize me. True, how many redheaded snowboarders could there be in Snowfall? But surely he didn't have me on the brain like I did him. In my puffy, figure-erasing snowboarding clothes, I was basically in drag.

And then he grumbled, "Get on the other side of me."

The snow squeaked under my head as I turned toward him. Was he talking to me?

He stood, grabbed the edge of my jacket in one hand and the edge of my snow pants in the other, and slid me five feet across the snow. He sat down again between me and the edge of the jump, like he was protecting me from rolling off. "Either do the jump or don't, Hoyden. In-between is very bad."

Some tourists up the hill yelled at us to get the hell out of the way. The boys scooted off one side of the jump, and Nick and I scooted off the other. Chloe stayed in the middle for a moment more. Clearly she preferred not to spend quality time alone with my brother and his friends. But when I made a small motion down by my side for her to join Nick and me, she shook her head and made a talking motion with her hand.

She wanted Nick and me to *talk*? Great. I huffed out one last sigh left over from my breathless moment hanging off the jump, and searched my mind for what I wanted to say to him. That I was sorry for insulting him about his parents splitting up, when I really didn't know? This would be difficult to explain, and I found myself hoping Chloe and/or Liz had played Telephone and passed this message along after all.

I looked up at him. He still had his goggles on, and so did I. If we removed them, we would be able to see each other better, but we would also see the face-divots that came with several hours of wearing goggles. So I left mine on, and so did he. When I tried to look into his eyes, all I saw was a reflection of snow, trees, and sky.

"You're welcome for saving your life." He grinned at me for the first time, and his playboy smile was all the more dazzling because that's all of him I could see—that and his strong chin—like he was a masked superhero. "Did Chloe say you were doing yoga?"

"Yeah, I help my mom teach a class at the health club," I said sheepishly. Nick could make me feel so happy about my own jokes, or so sheepish about the things that defined me. I loved and hated that about him.

"Does yoga help you levitate? Because it sure wasn't helping you climb back up that jump."

"It helps me stay focused so I can concentrate on tricks. It keeps me limber so I don't get hurt on hard landings. I could show you some stretches, now that you've decided you're this big boarder." Too late I realized this sounded like a come-on. *Yeah, Hayden,* he would say, *I want you to show me some*—wink—*stretches!*—nudge nudge.

"Stretches!" he barked in exactly the outraged tone he would use to say, *Pink sequined football uniforms!* "What good would that do?"

Now I was offended, which was strange because he hadn't even tried to offend me, for once. But stretches were a big part of my life. "Typical. High school boys think the only speed for exercise is full-throttle, with nothing between complete rest and heavy exertion. You're going to pull a muscle if you don't warm up enough."

"I warm up."

"Come on." I whacked his chest playfully, sugar-coating what I viewed as serious information. My insulated hand bounced off his insulated body. "I've seen the football team start practice. You're in full pads so you can hardly move, and you stretch what the coach tells you, when he says. You can't stretch right with a team. You're not listening to your own body."

"And *you* are? Tell me what my body's saying now." He flicked his long hair away from his goggles with his gloved pinkie. *God,* how I loved it when he did that. But he was plotting, scheming, turning my own words against me, making fun of me. He was *so hot*, even in goggles and waterproof layers, and I wished *so badly* he hadn't called me a bitch yesterday and insinuated I was a betty.

"No, you're right." I nodded. "What was I thinking? Yoga would be too hard for you. You're not subtle."

I almost cackled as his lips parted in surprise. Now that I'd discovered Nick's button, it was so easy to push! Just challenge him on *anything*. Tell him he couldn't do something. Press the button and watch him steam in the frigid air.

He leaned very close to me, his lips inches from my forehead. "Neither are you," he growled.

I flushed so hot that I was afraid he could see *me* steaming. What did he mean? Could he tell how much I liked him, after everything that had happened?

As quickly as he'd leaned toward me, he stepped away and glanced uphill. I turned to see what he was looking at. Gavin and Davis zigzagged down the mountain, barely missing each other each time they traded sides. As they approached the jump, they never hesitated. They both sped straight up the ramp and off the edge. Gavin recognized Chloe at the last second and called to her as he descended. Davis did a frontside 360, almost as if he'd seen me beside the jump and was mocking me, which was impossible because Davis did not mock people. Until last night, that is.

Then they were gone. Snowflakes sparkled in the air where they'd been.

Nick reached out and pulled my hair. "Don't worry," he whispered. "I won't tell Gavin and Davis about your incident with the jump just now."

I laughed shortly. "You mean you won't embarrass and belittle me? Thanks, Nick. It's too late. You took care of that last night."

He studied me for a second. At least, I thought he did, though all I could see were his mirrored goggles. Then his waterproof fabric zipped against my waterproof fabric as he slipped his arm around my shoulders. "Have fun out here with your boyfriends." He nodded across the slope to Josh and his posse, who were taking turns jibbing on the trick rail while the others pelted them with snowballs. Chloe protected her hairdo with both arms over her head.

I shrugged off his arm. "That's right. Fourteen-year-old boys have better taste than you. They think I'm *hot*." I licked my fingertip and stuck it on my butt. *"Tsssss."*

And with that, I propelled myself across

the slope and skidded to a stop at one end of the trick rail. "Quick," I told the boys, "act like you think I'm hot."

Chloe cracked up. Josh stared blankly at me. His friends blushed deep red, but they weren't claiming it.

"Thanks for your support," I told them. "Look without looking like you're looking. Is Nick gone?"

Chloe gazed past my shoulder to watch uphill. "He's hiking farther up so he can get some air. Here he goes."

"Nice speed," Josh murmured. All the boys tracked Nick behind me with their eyes. "Nice air." Josh turned to me. "You're toast."

I *felt* like toast, burning with anger inside my waterproof layers. "I am *not*," I insisted. "I might be lightly browned on one side. But it's only Wednesday. The comp isn't until Saturday. Right now let's go to the half-pipe and end this on a high note. Okay?"

I turned and boarded through the trees beside the jump without waiting for them. My enthusiasm was stretched to the limit, having to cheer on my own cheerleaders. Behind me Josh broke into a rap about me.

His friends joined in with beats and sound effects. I wasn't sure whether this was supposed to boost my spirits or not.

> Hayden, she's a red-haired lass
> Doing nose-grabs by the score
> Gonna kick some Krieger ass
> Maybe she needs one day more
> Wants to snowboard off the jump
> Not today, she's filled with sorrow
> Scared she'll lose her steeze and biff
> Gonna kick some ass tomorrow.

This was not exactly the vote of confidence I was looking for. I was already angry at myself for being chicken. I was glad I had something else to concentrate on—staying on the trail and not skidding into a tree—because otherwise, I might have burst into tears.

As soon as we cleared the woods and emerged onto the wide slope down to the half-pipe, Josh boarded even with me. "Your bet is only for Poser tickets, right?" he called.

And for my self-esteem, but that was splitting hairs. "Yeah, that's all."

"Because if it was for more than that, I'd

be sweet-talking Nick right now and doing everything I could to pull out."

"Oh, no you don't!" Chloe squealed. I think she meant to board between us and shove Josh away for effect. However, she didn't have enough control to do this, so she just crossed in front of him and fell in his path, which was somewhat anticlimactic. She shouted up at him, "*You* need to decide whether you stand with your sister or with the sexist pigs!" Even on her butt in the snow, Chloe was a formidable force.

"Yes, ma'am." Josh saluted with his mitten to his goggles, then slid around us to catch up with his friends, who had moved farther down the slope to the half-pipe. This was the part of the ski resort where everyone from my school came to see and be seen. The ski lodge sat at the foot of Main Street, the main wide slope. The half-pipe ended another big run on one side of Main Street. Kids busting ass in the pipe served as après-ski entertainment for adults drinking beer (and teenagers sneaking beer) on the deck at the lodge.

I stopped at the bottom of the half-pipe with twenty or thirty other skiers and boarders who were watching the show. Then

I turned to catch Chloe as she came down the hill. Over the years, on the rare occasions when she boarded with me, catching her had proven a more effective method of stopping her than teaching her to stop herself, which she could not seem to get the hang of.

In front of us, the guy who'd come in second place in the older boys' division yesterday sped through the pipe, which was basically the bottom half of a tube buried in the snow—an enormous tube with eighteen-foot sides. He boarded up one wall, launched into the air, and rotated his body in a backside 720. Then he landed easily and slid like butter down the wall, accelerating across the flat to launch himself up the opposite wall, back and forth until he ran out of pipe. He boarded out toward us. Seeing me on the edge of the crowd, he called, "Hayden O'Malley! My girlfriend and I have a bet for Poser tickets on you and Krieger. Be sure you lose that comp for me!"

Now that I looked around, there were a *lot* of people from school hanging out here, and all of them seemed to have heard about Nick and me. They murmured behind their hands or called out, "Dis!" and "Drama!" I even heard some girls close by discussing whether Nick and I were hooking up, as if I were deaf.

"You might as well fork over your seventy-two dollars right now!" Chloe yelled after the offending guy, but he was already halfway to the lift back up to the top of the pipe. To me she murmured, "You go almost as high as he does in the half-pipe. I don't want to scare you or anything. But you're sliding up the wall and going way up in the air, upside down half the time, and you're not the least bit scared of *that*. What's so different about the jump?"

I knew exactly what was so different, because I'd discussed this at length with Josh years ago when we first discovered I Did Not Do Jumps. "In the half-pipe I'm starting out in the flat, going up the wall and into the air, and then coming back down," I explained. "To me that's a lot different from the jump, which is basically a controlled fall off a very high wall. It sounds a little too much like equipment failure when you're rappelling."

"But you're *not* rappelling," Chloe pointed out, "and you don't have any equipment to fail you. Well, you have your snowboard, maybe, but no ropes or pulleys or whatever's supposed to hold you up. I have studied this in great detail today. While you were *not* going off the jump, everybody in Snowfall *did* go off it. My dentist. My mailman. An entire second grade class."

"What's your encouraging and helpful point, coach?" I prompted her.

"The jump's just mind over matter. It's *not* like you're falling off a cliff. When you go off the jump, you've got so much momentum that you fall gently, and the ground keeps sloping gently away from you as you go, so you have a longer ride." She demonstrated with her pink-gloved hands. One of them was the jump and the gentle slope. The other one was me, going off the jump and then falling to my death.

As if I needed instruction on this. As if I didn't live here in Snowfall and stare in awe at the jump every day of my life. "Thanks for the tip, professor. Okay, watch this." I turned around so I could see the jump behind us through the trees, and I put out my hands to spin Chloe around on her board. We watched a little kid go off the jump. "See how he loses his balance and moves his arms in wild circles like he's rolling down the windows on an old car? That means he's lost most of his balance and all of his control. I'm not going off anything where I might lose control. Ever. Again."

Chloe pushed her goggles off her face. Then she put both hands on the sides of my head and lifted my goggles so her blue eyes stared straight into my eyes. "Then you know exactly what you have to do. You have to take back control."

Midafternoon, I left the mountain. No loss there, since I didn't need any more practice at *not* going off the jump. I was scheduled to help my mom with yoga class. I didn't have the certification yet to teach yoga by myself. But we had a lot of elderly and disabled members at the health club, and my mom liked me to hang in the back of the class in case anyone needed special assistance. One time last year, she had to stop instruction when somebody got totally stuck in the Downward-Facing Dog.

On the hour, I walked into the main classroom and knelt in front of the stereo. I adjusted the music from the heinous

Sweatin'-to-the-Oldies aerobics beat for the class before ours to the calming ohm-like chords for yoga, complete with running water and chirping birds in the background. Out of the corner of my eye, I recognized all the regulars for this class and waved to them as they came in: new moms trying to lose the baby weight, a couple of men in rehab after skiing accidents, and old folks maneuvering slowly through the door, some with canes or walkers. Then came a few folks I didn't know, probably tourists who'd bought a temporary membership for their week or two in town. And then Nick.

Okay, it probably wasn't him. I was so angry with him that I had him on the brain and I was seeing him everywhere, just like I thought I saw him watching me from his deck during the competition yesterday. Oh, wait, that really *had* been him.

Anyway, I forgot all about phantom Nick when my mom bustled in. She liked to stay at the front desk, greeting guests, until the very last second, which was another reason she needed me there—to socialize before class and to set up the equipment for her. As I handed her the headset mic that would project her voice around the mirrored studio, she looked me up and down. "Well? Did you go off the jump?"

"Did she ever!" called an elderly lady at the back of the class. "Congratulations, Hayden! We saw your picture in the newspaper." Several people broke into applause.

My mother raised one eyebrow at me. "I haven't seen the paper today. Were you in the paper?"

"Uhhhhh." Without answering, I turned and hurried toward the back of the room, weaving around bodies on yoga mats in the center of the polished wood floor, thinking unkind thoughts about well-meaning old people who wanted to push me into being successful.

My mom got settled on the raised platform at the front of the class. She made her voice soothing as she coaxed everyone into Child's Pose. They curled into balls with their foreheads down on their mats and their arms out in front of them. I skirted one last mat to curl up on mine. Listening to my mom, I relaxed heavily into the pose. There was a reason I was so into yoga. I was high-strung (news flash!). Yoga helped me focus and keep a handle on what was important, so I didn't wig out over the small stuff. Only the big stuff.

Speaking of which, I followed my mom's instructions and slowly rose into Mountain Pose (that's standing up, if you want to get technical) and opened into Warrior One with one foot ahead. At the same time the man beside me, obviously a novice, got confused and held Warrior One with his other foot ahead. Mom moved us into Warrior Two, so our arms opened toward each other and I was able to glance at him out of curiosity without being obvious.

It really *was* Nick.

goofy

(gü 'fē) *adj.* **1.** riding the snowboard with your right foot forward, unlike most people **2.** Hayden, trying to act sophisticated

As I've said, Nick was no stranger to the health club. I'd whiled away many a shift behind the front desk, watching his love/hate relationship with the abdominal machine unfold on the surveillance cameras.

But he'd never, ever come to my mom's yoga class. When he'd showed up at the jump a few hours ago, I'd felt befuddled. Not angry, though. Not about *that*. He had as much right to the mountain as the rest of us, and he'd only happened upon us by accident.

Now I was angry. I supposed he had as much right as I did to use the health club, too, since his family was paying for a membership. I'd even told him this afternoon that I helped my mom with yoga. But after a fight like the one we'd had last night, he did *not* have a right to follow me to my family's business, to my *job*, insulting me.

He grinned at me and shook his dark hair out of his eyes. He was still holding Warrior Two and he didn't have a pinkie free to flick it. "You offered to show me some stretches," he murmured.

Not quietly enough. As my mom brought us up and around into Reverse Warrior with our arms pointed toward the ceiling, her calming yoga voice rose a notch.

The smart response would have been to ignore Nick—though this had never worked for me in the past. Instead, I said in a stage whisper, "You shouldn't have poked fun at my offer before, if it sounds like a good idea now."

"Return to Warrior Two," my mom intoned. "Breeeeeathe. You are strong like a warrior, with strong and stable roots down into the floor."

"I was being subtle." He wasn't facing me now. He directed his words forward, over his fingertips pointing ahead, with his perfect body in the perfect Warrior Two Pose. Except for, you know, the talking.

I did *not* speak over my perfectly pointed fingertips. Screw Warrior Two. I turned my head toward Nick, and it was all I could do to keep my arms out rather than putting my hands on my hips as I scolded him. "You don't care about yoga. You're here because I told you that you couldn't do it, and you can't *stand* to pass up a challenge."

My mom's soothing voice rose a bit more. "Open your body toward the wall, then sink into Triangle. Feel the stretch. Breeeeeathe. Continue to send strong and stable roots into the ground." This was her code for me to make sure the elderly people were not about to fall down.

I folded over into Triangle Pose. With my head hanging down, I looked through my legs straddled wide on the mat. The old folks appeared to me like they had pretty stable roots, or as stable as possible for hundred-year-olds doing yoga.

I glanced up at Nick, whose head was

very close to mine. His face was turning red.

"The Triangle Pose is not for everyone," I said drily.

Nick eyed me uneasily. Or maybe that was just the blood rushing to his head. Then he said, "You invited me here."

I shook my head, and my ponytails brushed the wood floor. "You misunderstood me. You were making fun of me for not going off the jump. Suggesting that you do yoga was my *subtle* way of telling you to go to hell."

"From here, move your hand behind your foot for Reverse Triangle. Breeeeeathe." My mom was practically shouting into her headset now. She might as well change the ohm-like yoga music with chirping birds to a nice, relaxing polka.

Reverse Triangle put Nick's head away from me, behind his muscular thigh. But even from several feet away, I heard him exclaim, "Ouch!"

"You think that hurt?" I asked out of the corner of my mouth. "Wait until Half Moon."

"Half Moon *does* hurt," someone nearby agreed. It was hard to tell who, with everyone upside-down.

"And roll up into Mountain Pose, with hands to heart's center." My mom stood, closed her eyes, and placed her hands in the prayer position on her chest. "Breeeeeathe and relax as two teenagers take a walk, leaving the haven of the yoga studio in peeeeeace and quiet." She opened one eye and lifted her eyebrow at me.

"Come on," I whispered to Nick. As my mom's voice droned on, I rolled up my yoga mat and whacked Nick in the back of the head with it. He looked up from his obviously painful Reverse Triangle and glared at me. Finally, he took the hint and rolled up his own mat. We wandered among the adults balancing precariously and dumped our mats into the bin by the door.

As soon as the door closed behind us, I whirled to face him in the hall. "Thanks, Nick. I've never been kicked out of my own yoga class before. My mom will probably dock me forty-five minutes of minimum wage."

He tilted his head to look at me from a different angle, and the scowl he'd been wearing since I'd whacked him in the head melted away. His words melted me in turn as he grinned brilliantly at me and said, "I really like your hair that way."

Without meaning to, I self-consciously reached for my hair. Around the health club, my mother always wore her red hair in one ponytail or one long braid down her back. I used to, too. But since I'd grown as tall as her, people mistook us for each other. I couldn't walk through the hall without middle-aged women stopping me to recount their hot flashes last night or to complain that the baby had the croup.

But I needed to pull my hair up for yoga, so I wore it in two ponytails. At first I worried the style was too little-girlish for me. Then, because of some of the looks I was getting from men at the health club who weren't regulars, I'd started to wonder whether the hairstyle had the opposite effect, reminding them of Britney Spears's schoolgirl getup.

Nick was giving me the same look. And this time, instead of being taken aback or feeling squicky about it, my heart raced and my face grew hot, my body's response to the call of Nick. The yoga music and my mother's soothing voice filtered through the door, reminding us we weren't exactly alone, and occasionally a lady in sequined track pants speed-walked past us in the wide hallway that doubled as an indoor track. But I couldn't stop glancing at Nick's soft lips. If a dark corner had been available, I would have kissed him right then, despite everything he'd said to me last night.

No, I would *not* let him charm me. I said, "Nick, for real. Why are you here? You didn't suddenly decide to pop into my mother's yoga class after four years of health club membership."

He still grinned at me with his head tilted, like he found me so amusing and did not take me seriously at *all*. Then he folded his arms on his chest, so his biceps strained at the sleeves of his T-shirt, courtesy of the arm curl machine. "Why can't I tell you you're pretty? You've got issues, Hoyden." He turned and walked into the men's locker room. The door closed gently behind him.

I stood in the hallway, listening to the muffled drone of my mother's voice, the slow yoga chords filtering through the studio walls, and the swish of the speed-walker's pants somewhere around the corner. I stared at the men's locker room door like my x-ray vision would switch on any second. Ugh, mistake— lots of our members came to the health club to get back into shape, with good reason. Still

I stared at the door, wondering what in the world was up with Nick. If he liked me, why was he mean to me? If he didn't like me, why did he show up here? Was it possible that Josh was right, and Nick's dis last night was a sign he actually had a thing for me? Again, this seemed very seventh grade. Maybe he was a case of arrested development.

Not in his biceps, of course. Or his abs. *Emotionally* arrested development.

The door burst open and I tensed like a rabbit, ready to bolt before Nick saw me staring at the door where he'd disappeared.

It wasn't even him. He hadn't had nearly enough time to shower. It was two regulars who walked out laughing and called a hello to me as they passed.

Swallowing the lump in my throat, I skittered into the women's locker room before Nick really did catch me staring. I'd wasted enough of my winter break worrying about Nick. I had plenty more to enjoy: no homework, meeting Chloe and Liz at Mile-High Pie for supper in a few minutes, lots of slope time, and a renewed push tomorrow to master the jump. Not for Nick's sake, but for mine.

As the locker room door thumped shut behind me, I pictured the lid closing on this box of troubles I'd opened with Nick's name on it. Unfortunately, when I emerged from the locker room again a few minutes later, ready for Mile-High Pie, Nick was standing in the hall in jeans and his puffy parka, talking with my mother.

Yoga class had let out. My mother was all about chatting up the members, even the teenagers, even the ones she kicked out of her classes (apparently). I ducked around them, into the crowd spilling out of the studio. Better let my mother cool down for a few hours before I faced her about interrupting her Reverse Triangle. I flounced down the staircase. With every step down, I felt myself relaxing a little more, looking forward to a few hours out with my girlfriends, away from Nick.

And then my mom called, "Have fun on your date, Hayden!"

Another step down and I thought, *Good. Mom is mistaken and has led Nick to believe I'm going on a date.*

One more step down and I thought, *Oh no, Mom has led Nick to believe I'm going on a date!* No matter how I tried to convince myself otherwise, obviously I still held out hope for Nick and me getting together this winter break. I turned around on the stair, wondering what I could say to let Nick know I was still unengaged, without letting him know I wanted him to know.

Nick ran smack into me.

"Ooof!" he hollered, grabbing me around the waist to keep me from falling down the rest of the staircase.

That's when I realized Mom thought Nick and I were going on a date *together*.

Quickly Nick let me go. He looked huge, frowning down at me from the step above. "Why are you stopping in the middle of the stairs?"

"Why are you tailgating me?"

He put his hand behind me, at butt level, without touching me. "*What* is *that*?" he demanded.

I bent a little and slapped my butt. "Something the heir to a meat fortune should know all about. USDA grade-A prime, baby." I straightened. "Just kidding. Really, it's my butt."

He put his hands on his hips, and from below I noticed his strong superhero chin again. He grumbled, "Why do you have 'boy toy' written across your butt?"

"Oh!" I put my hand over the words,

realizing that I probably should have been embarrassed about this sooner. "These are my little brother's jeans. He wrote it to annoy me. Or to get me a date. Speaking of which, what did you say to my mother to make her think we're going on a date?"

He shrugged. "I just told her we're both going to Mile-High Pie. Aren't you meeting Chloe and Liz there? I'm meeting Gavin and Davis."

More of Chloe and Liz's matchmaking, no doubt.

"Did you tell my mother that you called me a bitch last night, too?" I asked him. "Because that's the best way I know to win parents over."

For a split second, he looked uncomfortable. Almost immediately, he recovered and went back on the offensive. "You shouldn't wear those jeans. People might think something."

I stamped my foot on the stair. "Like what? I want to show off my fire-crotch? What do you care? God! Stop following me." My hair was down now, and I felt it smack into his chest as I whirled around and flounced down the rest of the stairs, across the lobby, and into the cold night.

I mean, *really* cold. The temperature must have dropped twenty degrees since I came off the slopes that afternoon. The formerly slushy snow on the lesser-used sections of the sidewalks had frozen over and now crunched under my boots. I tucked my nose deep into my scarf against a sudden gust of freezing wind. Mile-High Pie was only a few blocks away, but this walk seemed to stretch in front of me forever. Cold and anger were not a good mix.

"Hayden," Nick called from behind me.

Oh, good! Just what this walk needed: a double-shot of ex to go with that cold and anger. Shaking my head, I crossed the icy street.

"Hayden." His voice was sharper, angry now, and it echoed against the two-story storefronts closed for the night. I could tell from the direction of his voice that he was crossing the street after me.

"Don't you mean Hoyden?" I called over my shoulder.

Heavy steps cracked behind me, closer and closer. Nick rounded in front of me and stood in my path, his breath puffing white into the black night. "I never called you that."

"You call me Hoyden all the time!"

He frowned at me and said, "Fire-crotch."

"Take a number." I tried to walk around him.

He caught me by the elbow. "Would you hold up for a minute and listen to me?" His dark eyes focused on me, hardly blinking when the wind gusted in his face. He put on a very convincing act of disbelief and outrage. "I mean, I did *not* call you a fire-crotch. I was afraid you overheard that in the lunchroom last week. *Everett Walsh* called you a fire-crotch as you walked by. I told Everett Walsh that he should watch his mouth. Then Everett said, 'Oh, you're one to talk, you say stuff like that about Hayden all the time,' and I said, 'I would *never* make a comment about her *crotch*. No.' We nearly got into it right there in the lunchroom, but you conveniently missed *that* part."

I certainly had. And I wasn't buying it. Nick, standing up for me? "Let me get this straight. Your lunchroom speech went a little something like this." I put my hands out in front of me like I was a Roman orator enunciating for the crowd. "'I, Nick Krieger, defender of women, would never denounce the crotch. I am *above* the crotch.'"

He gaped at me. Other boys might not look so hot while gaping. Nick looked adorable in the soft light of the streetlamps, against a backdrop of small town and snow.

I put my hands down.

He watched me silently for a few moments more. "You don't think very well of me," he finally said.

I shrugged. "I don't blame you for being confused and thinking, 'Gosh, I called Hayden a fire-crotch and she's *mad*? What's up with *that*?' There was a time in my life when you could have called me a fire-crotch in front of a bunch of people, and I would have just laughed. I wanted any kind of attention I could get from you. In eighth grade, ninth grade, tenth grade, when you insulted me and other girls said it was just because you liked me, I believed it. But I guess everybody reaches a point when they're done with that, and they want to be respected. This is definitely unfortunate for the purposes of teen love—I mean, look at Gavin. But there it is."

"You don't want to be with me because you think I don't respect you."

"I *know* you don't respect me."

"Because you don't believe me that I didn't call you a fire-crotch?"

"You don't have a good track record for telling me the truth." I walked around him and nuzzled my nose into my scarf again, heading into the wind.

His boots crunched behind me.

"And stop following me!" I yelled over my shoulder.

"I'm not following you. Stop walking in front of me." The crunches sounded louder and louder again until he jogged past me and kept jogging until he was fifty feet ahead of me on the sidewalk. He disappeared around the corner. I was left with nothing but my anger and the cold again.

When I finally reached the restaurant and swung open the door, of course the first thing I saw was Nick hanging his parka on the coatrack, revealing how adorable he looked in his sweater and scarf underneath. And Fiona Lewis was calling to him from the ancient Galaga arcade game. His *other* ex. Drat!

"Haaaaaydeeeeen!" moaned Josh and his peeps from the nearest booth. Double drat! Just what I needed when I was trying to get the upper hand in this ongoing argument with Nick: the undying friendship of four fourteen-year-old boys.

On hearing my name, Nick looked up at me, then nodded toward the posse with a smirk. "Your boyfriends are calling you." He glanced toward Fiona.

"You act like that's not possible," I heard myself say coyly, even though my brain was waving frantically at me, screaming, *Stop, Hayden, don't go there!*

Nick turned back to me, and his eyes flew wide in surprise. "I act like *what's* not possible?"

"You act like I would never go out with any of them." Which I wouldn't. They were like brothers to me. Especially my brother. And they still watched cartoons. It was just that Nick acted so *disdainful*, as if I could never have anyone if it weren't for him or Everett Walsh throwing me a bone.

"Nick, quick, help, I'm about to die!" Fiona squealed.

Ah, triple drat. A real live ex-girlfriend and damsel in space-distress totally trumped fourteen-year-old boys, no matter how many of them there were. Nick dashed over to her and took over mission command. I hung my own coat on the rack and dragged myself to the boys' booth.

But you know what? They all grinned at me in welcome, and Josh even scooted over to make room for me on the bench. At least I knew who my true friends were. Feeling grateful and loved, I sat down.

THPPPPTHPPPPTHPPPPT! I farted. Or so it seemed.

The boys died laughing. I pulled the whoopee cushion out from under me and flung it on the table, which only sent them into another paroxysm.

"Nick——Krieger——is——behind——you," Josh gasped between giggles. "He totally heard it over Galaga. Do you still want us to look without looking like we're looking?" This sent them into yet another laughing fit.

"But don't worry," one of his friends said. "We'll act like we think you're hot." They all snorted and dabbed at their eyes faux-girlishly with paper napkins from the holder. Then, as if on cue, they started their rhythmic heavy breathing, and I knew one of Josh's raps was coming. The people in the booths around us turned to look, if they weren't already staring at us outright because of the whoopee cushion.

Hayden C. O'Malley was your
Average girl
Thought she'd give the boarding, jibbing,
Riding a whirl
Thought she'd have some trouble kicking
Nick Krieger's ass
But her secret weapon is she's
Cooking with gas . . .

Not every one of Josh's raps was a success, and this one trailed off to dissolve in a
morass of laughter and fart noises. I laughed
along with them, because it was funny, and
because I was that much of a Loser.

But of course the whole time I was preoccupied, wondering whether Nick had
gone home with Fiona yet. On the one
hand, I hoped that the two of them got
extra points and extra lives in the bonus
round, and that they were sticking around
for another hundred thousand points. On
the other hand, Nick overhearing Josh's rap
would not be my shining moment.

"Do you think y'all could hold it down?"
I finally asked the boys. "I appreciate your
art, but there's a difference between rapping
about me on the slopes, and rapping about
me in a restaurant where other people are

trying to eat. The latter is very prepubescent."

"*Pre*pubescent!" Josh gasped. "*Pre*-pubescent!"

"I am totally pubescent," one of his friends said.

Another said haughtily, "I will have you know that my mom and I are going to Aspen to shop for training bras this weekend."

I rolled my eyes. "Later." I slid off the bench and stood.

"Hey, we're helping you go off the jump again tomorrow, right?" Josh asked, using the word *helping* very loosely.

"Yeah," another boy said, "eleventh time's the charm."

I looked toward the Galaga machine. Fiona was still there, yet Nick was gone. Probably just to order her a drink. Ordinarily, I would have bounced all over the restaurant searching for him so I could flirt him out of Fiona's pink-nailed grasp. But the whoopee cushion had taken the wind out of my sails.

As I walked through an open doorway decorated with broken skis and snowboards, here he was again, sitting in a booth, handsome face lit softly by the dim overhead lamps and the Christmas lights outlining the ceiling. Colors danced in his dark hair as he laughed with Gavin and Davis and . . . Chloe and Liz.

Sure enough, Chloe and Liz had invited me here, Gavin and Davis had invited Nick, and they were all playing Cupid again. Even after the fiasco last night! But I knew for sure that either way, the couples were back together, at least for tonight. Chloe and Gavin sat on one side of the booth, and I saw the backs of Liz and Davis on the other side. Nick had squeezed onto the end of the bench next to Gavin, which left only one place for me.

My feet felt like they had boots and bindings and two separate snowboards attached to them as I dragged myself closer and closer to the table of doom. Nick looked up at me. He didn't sneer at me and turn away to make a joke about me to the table at large. He watched me coming, dragging my phantom snowboards across the room. I held his gaze. I knew he was about to humiliate me (again), but I would hold my head high while he did it. I slid onto the bench next to Davis, across the table from Nick.

"Hayden!" Chloe said. "Where've you been?"

I jerked my head in the direction of my brother. "Josh."

Here it came. Nick offered another explanation with a smug grin. "Hayden's having gastrointestinal issues."

"You are?" Liz asked with real concern.

"Must be the tofu," I muttered. When Liz continued to stare at me with wide eyes, I reached around Davis and patted her hand. "No, I'm not. Nick is kidding. Isn't he hilarious?" I gave him a sickly smile.

He pointed at himself like, *Who, me?*

Conversation at the table went on without us. Gavin related the details of the trip to Japan his family was planning for next summer to visit relatives they hadn't seen in years. Even if Liz and Chloe hadn't completely made up with Davis and Gavin, it was so obvious they were couples, because they sat next to each other in the booth. I felt a flash of jealousy. Maybe it was just that the bet for Poser tickets loomed over me, but I couldn't shake the idea of all six of us triple-dating.

What if Nick and I were a real couple for once, out in the open? Nick and I would slide together onto the bench on one side of the booth, and all our friends would take it for granted. He'd been cruel to hint around at asking me out when he didn't mean it, because now I couldn't get it off my mind.

As if he knew what I was thinking, he startled me by pushing the big plate of community nachos in front of me. "No wonder you're so skinny," he said quietly. "Why aren't you eating?"

"Hayden's a vegetarian," Liz called across the table.

"Oh yeah, I forgot." Nick gave me a perplexed look, like he'd just found out I was a nun or a spy.

"How can you have gone to school with her for four years and not known that?" Liz challenged him. "Why do you think she's the only person who brings her lunch on pepperoni pizza day at school?"

Davis could not get his brain around it. "Is it some Tennessee granola health club thing?"

"Just a granola health club thing," I explained. "My family didn't go vegetarian until right before we left Tennessee." Luckily, I wasn't the least bit self-conscious about being a vegetarian, because I knew it was good for me. If I'd been self-conscious, I might have begun to get uncomfortable right about then. With one short, unpainted fingernail, I traced a heart carved into the thick wooden table.

It was Gavin's turn to look perplexed. "You're from Tennessee?"

"Of course she's from Tennessee," Nick said. "Why do you think we always make fun of her accent?"

Gavin shrugged. "Because it's there?"

Davis laughed and choked on his water. Liz pounded him on the back while Chloe commented, "Somebody's being made fun of and you come running, no matter who or why, right?"

Gavin and Davis simultaneously said, "Right."

"But I forgot you were a vegetarian," Nick repeated to me. "I offered you nachos exactly like that in seventh grade, at this very table. You said you were a vegetarian and I nearly died of embarrassment for offering you meat."

"And meat products," Gavin couldn't help chiming in.

But after Gavin's comment, conversation stopped, and everyone stared at Nick. Nick? Dying of embarrassment?

He must have realized he'd blown his suave cover, because his face turned bright red.

Nick? Turning red?

"Excuse me," I said, sliding off the bench. "I'm going to the ladies' room." I was a peeless goddess no longer. That was so seventh grade. Now I was in eleventh grade, and I peed. Though of course I didn't need to at the moment. I needed to confer with my girlfriends.

"Me, too!" Chloe and Liz both said. The boys stood to let them out. Gavin and Davis grumbled about girls always having to go to the bathroom together. Nick never took his eyes off me. He knew my need to pee was a total put-on.

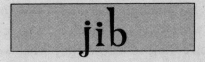

jib

(jib) *v.* **1.** to board around and over obstacles **2.** such as Nick

Without waiting for the girls, I rushed between the booths and down a dark hall to the tiny women's bathroom, which was wallpapered with women's wipeouts. Big photographs cut out of the newspaper, pictures cut from magazines, and snapshots showed women on skis (and a few more recent shots of women on snowboards) taking hard spills and kicking up snow. Usually I found the bathroom highly amusing. Today, as soon as I opened the door, I stopped short. The walls were sending me a message.

But I didn't stand there in awe for long, because Chloe burst through the door behind me. I hollered at her, "You're trying to set me up with Nick again!"

"We are *not*," Chloe insisted, moving over to let Liz through the door. "We thought about what you said last night. You're right. We don't want to throw away what we have with Gavin and Davis. So we thought we'd meet them here and reconcile. *Without* giving up those Poser tickets."

I folded my arms. "And you just happened to forget about that when you invited me, too? And Gavin and Davis just happened to forget they were meeting you when they invited Nick?"

Chloe tossed her blond hair and said, "Yes."

"No," Liz sighed, "we *are* trying to set you and Nick up."

Chloe glared at Liz. "Remind me never to embezzle any funds with you. The least bit of pressure and you crack!"

"It's not right to hide it from her." Liz turned to me. "I definitely have misgivings about you getting together with Nick after that fire-crotch business in the lunchroom on Thursday."

"Ah, update," I said, turning a bit red myself. "He said I was wrong about that. I didn't believe him at the time, but . . ." Something in Nick's dreamy expression when he'd mentioned the seventh grade just now had made me wonder. Was it possible that he *had* defended me against Everett Walsh? It was all sort of medieval and chivalrous and romantic if I didn't think too hard about it.

Liz nodded. "See, we may have been underestimating Nick. I feel responsible." She leaned back against the wall. Her shoulders just covered an enlargement of a girl snowboarder in the midst of a spectacular face-plant. "Gavin and every other boy in school ribbing Nick about you . . . that all started in seventh grade. Remember that awful night at the Will Smith movie, right after you'd moved here?"

"Vaguely." I rubbed my thumb across two chicks crashing into each other on skis as if I were getting bored with this convo.

"*I* remember," Chloe called out. "I was trying to balance a couple of boyfriends at once. I had a *lot* to learn about cheating."

Liz stared blankly at Chloe for a moment, then turned back to me.

"Will Smith movie," I reminded her.

Liz shook her curls. "Right. I've always regretted telling you that Nick and Gavin had a bet about you. Nick had asked everyone not to tell you. Nobody wanted to go against what Nick said. But I couldn't leave you out there alone, not knowing." She shifted uncomfortably against the wall, like the snowboard in the picture was jabbing her between the shoulder blades. "I've been the butt of jokes before."

I looked from Liz to Chloe and back to Liz. "Then why do you regret telling me?"

"I'm not sure anymore that he meant it as a joke," Liz said.

"How else could he have meant it?" I shrieked. I looked to Chloe for help in talking Liz out of this insanity. But Chloe just poofed up her blond hair in the mirror, almost as if she agreed with Liz about this.

Liz shrugged. "I know Nick has a funny way of showing it, but I honestly think he's got it bad for you. Chloe thinks so, too."

Chloe nodded her affirmation. "So do Gavin and Davis. Seventh grade to eleventh grade—that's a long time to go out of your way to be mean to somebody you can't stand."

I didn't say it, but surely Liz and Chloe felt what I felt: a vibration shaking the bathroom and speeding up my heart rate at the thought that Nick really liked me. I could *not* fall for this and get hurt again, but Nick was so tempting. I wished it were true.

Feeling dizzy, I backed against the wall beside Liz for support. "This is why I wanted to talk to you chicks in here. I'm sure that, against my instructions, you told Davis and Gavin to tell Nick that I didn't know his parents were separated, right?"

They eyed each other and nodded.

"But has he apologized for calling me a bitch? No. He came to my mother's yoga class just now, and we argued about that. Then we argued about the fire-crotch business. Now he's sitting across from me at a booth in Mile-High Pie, waxing poetic about the seventh grade. He's basically followed me around all day and poked at me, without an apology in sight." I whacked the back of my head on the pictures of snowboarders in mid-fall.

Liz gazed at me, wide-eyed and awestruck. "Wow. He's *definitely* smitten. He wants to apologize, but he doesn't know how to approach you because *you're* mad, which makes him madder and madder."

"You know what I think?" Chloe asked. She was going to tell me whether I wanted to know or not. "I think you've both built up enormous amounts of sexual tension since your session in the sauna was cut short last night, and you won't get along until you let it out. You need to make out with him. Take control."

Before I could pursue this astonishing idea with her, three senior girls pushed through the bathroom doorway and squealed when they saw me. "Hayden O'Malley!" one of them said. "I had a huge fight with my boyfriend about you, and we both joined the bet over Poser tickets. I think every couple in the school has made that bet with each other. You'd better show that boy up."

"I heard you and Nick are actually hooking up," another girl said. "Is that true?"

Chloe nodded at me encouragingly. Liz motioned with her head toward the door.

"I'm not sure. Let me get back to you." I swung open the bathroom door and walked into the restaurant again. This was my evening out: bopping back and forth, away from whichever convo made me the most uncomfortable.

I walked back to the booth and stood next to Nick. He was leaning forward, listening to what Davis and Gavin were saying. I waited for them to finish. I stood naked beside him—wearing BOY TOY jeans, a long-sleeved shirt, and a short-sleeved PowderRoom.net T-shirt over that, but feeling naked nevertheless—for several long seconds.

When he finally noticed me, he looked up quickly like he'd been waiting on edge for my return. He set down his pizza, crumpled his napkin in his hands, and even slid his half-filled plate toward the center of the table like *I* was the main course now and he was making room for me. "So, Hoyden."

I noticed the Christmas lights glinting in his dark hair again, reflecting in his dark eyes. It took me a moment to remember I had something to tell him. Nick had that effect on me.

I bent down and cupped my hand around his ear—such an intimate gesture on its own. The coarse strands of his hair brushed my fingers as I whispered, "Chloe and Liz think we need to make out."

I jumped away at his sudden movement. He leaped up from the table and grabbed my hand. "I'll get my coat."

"What's your hurry?" Gavin called after us, but Nick didn't stop pulling me through the room. Booth after booth of loving couples flashed by, along with the wooden columns that divided the booths, each covered in years of graffiti: ALEX LOVES TAYLOR. CATHY + DAN. SYDNEY ♥s BRANDON. We flew at light speed through the restaurant, going back in time to that magical seventh grade night, and I couldn't help giggling.

I did have some misgivings as we approached the door. But Fiona had left the Galaga machine. I never should have felt jealous about her. If Nick went out with her again, that would have been *four* dates, which was unheard of for him. And Josh and his posse had left their table. They must have gone down to the movie theater, where they could humiliate middle school girls with the whoopee cushion. I made a mental note to explain to Josh that this would not bring him any closer to a date with Gavin's sister, either.

Nick looked for his coat on the rack. I snagged mine and shrugged it on without stopping. I swung open the front door of the restaurant. The frigid night wind blew snow into my eyes.

"Hayden," Nick called to me.

"Close the door," hollered the couples in the booths nearest us.

I let go of the door handle, then turned to Nick in the warm room. When he just stood there, staring down at me, I walked back to him.

"On second thought," he said, "I don't know about this."

I was *not* going to get dissed again. I said brightly, "Oh, don't be scared. It's easy!" I jerked his puffy parka down from the rack and held it open for him. "Try one arm at a time."

Glaring at me, he took the coat and shrugged it on. "Close the door!" shouted the couples around us as we walked outside.

Now that my eyes were used to the lights indoors, the night was black, except for the streetlights glowing yellow, and the dark blue mountain looming over the downtown buildings. Blinking the snowflakes out of my eyes, I took Nick's warm bare hand in mine and dragged him along the narrow path down a sidewalk that had been cleared of snow. I turned in at the alley between Mile-High Pie and an antiques store next door, closed for the night. The snow was deep here, and the alley was empty and dark.

"Hayden," he said softly. He slumped a bit against the brick wall and—oooh—did the pinkie-flick to his hair. But it wasn't to get me hot. In fact, he'd cooled quite a bit since I'd first whispered in his ear.

"Let's talk." I reached up to touch his shoulder, showing him I had no hard feelings that he'd lost the mood. "Gavin and Davis told you I didn't know about your parents when I made those comments last night, right?"

He nodded shortly. His hair fell back into his eyes. "Right."

"But you still haven't apologized for calling me a bitch and dissing my contest win."

"I know, and I'm sorry."

Chloe had been right! If I let Nick control our conversation, we followed each other around, throwing insults all night. Yet the second I took control, I finally got the apology I'd needed to forgive him.

Or so I thought. Then he added, "But what you said to me in the sauna was really mean, considering."

I folded my arms across my thick coat. "I understand that, *now*. But I know, and now you know, that I *didn't* understand what was going on at your house when I said that."

"Right."

I studied his handsome face. Even now, the uneducated observer would say he looked happy. Only I saw his slightly narrowed eyes and heard the edge in his voice. "You're still mad at me anyway," I said. "*I'm sorry I called you a bitch, but* doesn't count as an apology."

He put up one hand to wipe away the tiny snowflakes sticking and melting in the stubble on his chin. "You don't know how mad I was at you in the first place. I think I've done really well to back down as far as I have. Chloe and Liz say I should ask you out. Everybody in school had been telling me that, actually. But when it came down to it, in the hall last Friday, you made that comment about your lawyer. I thought you might say no and rub my face in it."

Exactly what I'd thought. If he might lose, he didn't want to play.

"My parents argued the whole weekend,"

he said. "I was pretty much home for the entire thing, except when I was boarding. It's been coming on for a while, but I couldn't help thinking I'd brought it on somehow by making those divorce jokes to you in the hall on Friday."

"Oh." I might believe in a little karma to go with my yoga, but Nick hadn't done anything to deserve *that*. I wanted to wrap my arms around him to comfort him. I didn't touch him, though. I didn't dare.

He splayed his hands on his jeans and rubbed his thighs like he could hardly stand to stay in his own skin any longer. "Then, in the sauna, I got a second chance to ask you out. I was really into what we were doing— or, as it turns out, not doing."

"You never did ask me out," I reminded him.

"I was *going* to. I thought we would get together. And then, when you said I never take you anywhere, and I take you for granted, and I ignore you except when it's convenient, you sounded almost exactly like my mother yelling at my father right before she left."

That hurt. I knew I hadn't said those things to him. But coming off a whole weekend of listening to his parents bicker, that's what he must have heard when I'd said he hadn't asked me to the Poser concert, he hadn't congratulated me on winning the boarding contest, and he only wanted to be with me now that our friends were together. I actually grimaced at a pain in my stomach at the thought I'd hurt him so much. "Nick—"

He waved away what I was about to say. "I'm sorry. I know that's not what you wanted to hear, and it's definitely not sexy, but I wanted you to understand what happened. I'd told Gavin and Davis some of what went down with my parents, so I figured you could have known. If you were throwing that back in my face, you were a different person than I thought. I've probably never been that angry at anyone in my life. Except my dad." He bit his lip, looking so unsure and so much younger, for once, than seventeen. "I know that's not fair to you. I'm going through kind of a tough time right now, and I might not be thinking straight."

"It's okay." I shuffled forward through the snow to hug him, whether he wanted to be hugged or not. As Chloe had said,

Nick needed my support. As a friend. All our arguments seemed silly now, compared with what he'd been going through at home.

To my surprise, he put both his arms around me and hugged me closer, until I had to step toward him on the icy pavement. His body curved around me. I felt his hot breath in my hair, and I shivered.

"Are you cold? Here." He unzipped his jacket, then unzipped mine—my heart was doing flips as his hands passed down my chest, unzipping me—and he pulled me even farther forward, into his body heat.

I'd been shivering from the feelings he stirred in me every time he looked at me, not from the cold. But I certainly was not going to clue him in if he wanted to share bodily warmth. Sometimes it was best to leave well enough alone. His 98.6-degree body was an 80-degree contrast to the cold night all around me. My heart sped up, pumping my confused blood so hard through my veins that I could hear it in my ears.

"So Chloe and Liz think we should make out." He spoke just above a whisper. The low notes of his voice made my insides quiver.

I looked way up at him, into his dark eyes. "Well, last night we didn't finish what we started." I put my hands in his hair and drew his face down toward mine, enjoying every second of anticipation, feeling the aura of heat around him. I kissed his neck, just below his chin.

In yoga class, I could see when people started to let go of their busy schedules and relax into the stretches. Now I could feel Nick leave Mile-High Pie behind, and the snowy street, and the cold mountain, and relax into this little cloud of warmth with me. "God, Hayden," he breathed.

I kissed my way across his neck. He blindly fumbled under my jacket until his hot hand slid inside my T-shirt. He took my chin in his other hand and turned my face toward his, looking me all over, my eyes, my hair, my lips. I thought for a moment he was going to tell me to stop.

And then he kissed me, softly at first, then more firmly and deeply. He was not going to tell me to stop. His second thoughts were gone. He was fully committed, at least to this make-out session. His tongue swept deep inside my mouth. He gathered fistfuls of my T-shirt on either side of my waist and held me tight. For long minutes, as the cold wind teased us outside our cocoon of coats, we warmed each other and breathed each other.

It went on for thirty minutes, I would say. I'm really not sure. Time flew when I was having fun, but my brain recorded every tiny detail of his mouth on mine like we were moving in slow motion in the hot air. Like I was falling off a cliff.

Finally, when I was absorbed in the sensations of my own body and his, and I'd totally forgotten anything but the two of us in this hot moment, he brought me back. He took his hands away, broke the kiss, and stood up straight. Snow squeaked under his boots as he shifted his weight. "Do you realize we've been standing here making out in the snow and the fifteen-degree weather for five minutes?"

"Five?" I asked in a daze, touching my tingling lips and staring dumbly up at him.

"Can we go to your house?" he purred in a sexy voice.

Boy, could we! I couldn't wait to get him into my warm living room. I wasn't ready for the tingles to end, and Nick's lips on mine *plus* climate control sounded too good to be true. But I wanted to get one thing straight first. "Does this mean we're calling off the bet?"

He frowned down at me. "Of course we're not calling off the bet. You owe me a Poser ticket. Did you only come out here to get me to call off the bet?"

I sighed and looked up at the stars in exasperation. But I stopped short of walking away from him, just in case he came to his senses and decided to kiss me again. I found one of his hands and held it, gently stroking his palm with my thumb, toying with his signet ring. Feeling a little like Fiona or some other girl from my school whose voice seemed to pitch an octave higher whenever she wanted something from a boy, I asked, "Why do you want to be with me if you think so little of me?"

"I'm not sure I do want to be with you." He slid his hand out of mine. Devastating as that was, he floored me with what he did next. He faced me again and gave me the brilliant smile with the movie-star expression he always wore around school. As if none of this had happened at all. He walked by me, away from the wall, through the deep snow to the sidewalk, and disappeared around the corner of the building.

I stared into the space where he'd been, an alley entrance filled with tiny snowflakes. My tummy still swirled with tingles like the snowflakes in the air. How could Nick and I be over as suddenly as we'd started? Sure, I'd wanted him to call off the bet now that we were together. I'd expected him to. But that's not why I'd come out here with him. Truly wheedling something out of a boy, Fiona-style, required planning and organizational skills that I did not possess.

"Hoyden," Nick called from around the corner.

I shuffled after him through the snow. He had one hand on the door of Mile-High Pie, prepared to open it for me.

"I'm going home," I told him. No way was I sitting at a booth in Mile-High Pie again tonight. When I got home I would call Chloe and then Liz. They would ask if Nick and I had gotten together. I would say that for a second there, I thought we were going to, but . . . then I asked him to forfeit a challenge. I could explain all this to them on the phone, but I did not want to rehash it at the table, or in the bathroom. Mile-High Pie was a dangerous place.

"Got a ride?" he asked in exactly the polite but distant tone he would use on some ninth grader he hardly knew.

"Bus." I gestured toward the familiar squeaks as the bus lumbered around the corner several blocks down.

"Okay, then. See you around, Hoyden." He pulled the door open.

"Close the door!" called the couples as he stepped inside.

I watched him through the glass door as he hung up his puffy parka, then wove between the tables and slipped into the booth where we'd been sitting. He nodded at something Gavin said to him. But Nick's shoulders were hunched, and he looked so defeated that I wanted to hug him again. I wished I didn't feel so strongly that he shouldn't have challenged me to this comp. I wished he would run back out to me, tell me it was all a joke, and make out with me against the wall like he was supposed to.

Watching Nick's defeated pose, I realized that wasn't going to happen. Nick might have enjoyed making out with me.

He might even want to be with me. But more than anything, Nick wanted to win. And winning me over wasn't enough.

"Hayden! Yoo-hoo, Hayden O'Malley! Are you and Nick Krieger finally hooking up?"

"How are these people recognizing me?" I muttered to Liz beside me. We'd just slid away from the top of a ski lift, one I could stand to ride because it never rose too far from the ground, when we were overtaken by sophomores. It was snowing—not a pleasant light shower with the sun occasionally breaking through the clouds, either, but a heavy, constant dump from overcast skies that made visibility almost nil. Without admitting it, I'd had an eye out for Nick all day, and I figured Liz had been looking for Davis, but we'd never recognized them in the thick white air. Yet these sophomores were the fifth group of boarders from our school to pick me out that afternoon. My hair must glow in the dark.

"Dish, Hayden," exclaimed a gossip-seeking girl who skied directly into my path. "It would be sooooo cute if you and Nick got together after he sealed your backpack inside that plaster of Paris volcano last year."

Liz giggled and elbowed me. "I'd forgotten all about that one!"

"But my friends say no way," the girl went on. "Nick hates you. Which is it?"

I shrugged. "I guess you'll have to ask Nick." And if she found out, I hoped she'd pass that info along to *me*.

"Practice hard," said another girl shooting past on her board. She called backward to me, "I've got a Poser ticket riding on you."

"Me, too!" said another girl accelerating down the white slopes. "Me, too! Me, too!" more of them called, until the air was as thick with pressure as it was with snowflakes.

Liz knew what I was thinking. "Let it go," she advised me. "We're taking the afternoon off, remember?"

We'd worked hard all morning at getting me to go off the jump, with no success, despite the "help" of Josh and his posse. On the bright side, if I never became a professional snowboarder and never opened that door for Josh, he already had a whole album's worth of raps about me, my boarding, and my gastrointestinal issues. Maybe he could sign a record contract.

But Liz and I had made a pact that no matter what happened this morning, we would let loose this afternoon and have fun on the mountain. Much as I loved Chloe, she was a pain to board with, because I was forever slowing down so she could keep up, or helping her right herself and innocent bystanders after she crashed into the ski-lift line. To be honest, I was relieved she'd said she couldn't board with us today because she had "a pressing matter to attend to," even though her tone of voice made me suspicious she was meddling in my business again. Liz was a different story completely. On her skis, Liz kept up with me.

"Why don't we go down Main Street?" She gestured to the enormous slope in front of us with the ski lodge a tiny dot at the bottom. "And then we'll have time to take the lift up for one last run before it gets dark."

"Race ya," I said, getting a five-second head start on her before she could put her goggles down.

We crisscrossed the expanse of snow. She leaped over moguls and crash-landed on the other side, her falls cushioned by six inches of fresh powder. I used the moguls to launch me into lazy 360s. We giggled and shouted and nearly ran into each other a dozen times on our way down. Despite the slow powder conditions and the snow plastering my goggles so I had to stop and wipe them every few minutes, this was what snowboarding was really about for me. Speeding downhill in a race was fun, and I loved pushing my body to land new stunts with steeze. But the real joy came in messing around with friends, exploring, trying new things without worrying about how they'd look, and knowing I could come back and do it all again tomorrow.

"Boy alert," Liz called as we reached the bottom of Main Street and passed the half-pipe. I stopped beside her, shook the snow out of my hair (gingerly, because the ends of my hair were heavy with ice), and pulled off my goggles so I could see. Sure enough, Nick, Davis, and Gavin stood in line on the side of the pipe, waiting their turns and watching another guy bust ass on a 720 attempt.

"Oooh," said the crowd around the pipe.

"Oooh," echoed the people braving the snow to drink beer or hot chocolate out on the deck of the ski lodge. They were far enough away that their voices reached us a split second later.

"Do you want to go and say hi to the boys?" Liz asked me. She was so sweet to ask me first. I *knew* she wanted some Davis time since she hadn't seen him all day, but I'd told her how things had ended last night between me and Nick.

"Sure," I told her. "I have to go back to school with Nick on Monday. No point in avoiding him now." She took off her skis and I kicked off my board below the pipe, and we hiked up behind the boys in the center of the crowd of spectators lining the lip.

"Davis," Liz called.

He looked back toward us, ducked his head so he could see us among the other spectators, and waved at us. Then he turned around to the half-pipe again. He and Gavin both leaned their heads in toward Nick so all three of them could share a laugh. I heard their cackles echo against the far side of the half-pipe. The whole crowd sighed, "Oooh." And then I heard Nick say, "Fire-crotch."

biff

(bif) *n.* **1.** crash **2.** somebody bites it

Thinking back on it later, I realized I must have dropped my board without any regard to how far away it might have slid down the slope. I must have climbed to the rim of the half-pipe with surprising nimbleness, considering my usual trouble maneuvering in my boarding boots. I must have pushed five people aside. But all I remember is shoving Nick in the back and screaming, "Liar!"

He spun around with his dark eyes wide. It was the only time I'd ever seen him startled.

"Did you call me a fire-crotch in the

lunchroom, Nick?" I shouted. "Did you? Does it really matter if you didn't, when you called me one just now? You have got a lot of freaking nerve!" Panting, I managed to stop myself from saying anything else, because so many people around us were leaning in, listening, murmuring about the bet and the Poser concert.

But what I'd said didn't begin to tap how furious I was with him, and how hurt I was. He'd stood there in the snow at Mile-High Pie last night and made me feel sorry for him! He'd made me feel terrible for something I didn't even do, after he'd lied to me to my face! And then he'd kissed me, and I'd let him!

Mortifying.

Now his lips parted. I waited to hear the next lie. I almost hoped it was a good one, so at least I'd have an entertaining story to share with my friends about what an ass he was.

But Davis spoke up first in a reasonable tone, like a psychiatrist soothing a loony. "We weren't talking about you, Hayden."

Gavin jerked his thumb over his shoulder. "The kid in the pipe just busted his nuts on the deck."

I glared at Gavin, showing him I didn't buy his ridiculous story. Then, just to make sure he was lying, too, I stuck my head between him and Nick and peered into the pipe. A freshman lay at the bottom of the course, holding his crotch. As I watched, he slowly stood and used his board as a crutch to hobble out of the pipe. The spectators cheered like he was an injured football player walking off the field during a game.

Nick was watching me. Not glaring. Just watching me with an expression beyond hurt.

I took a breath, and couldn't think of anything to say.

"Come on, Nick," Gavin called. "You're up. Better get your head in the game, if you know what I mean."

Nick still watched me as he passed. Then all three boys turned their backs on me as they hiked above the pipe. Nick stepped onto his board and lowered his goggles.

"Here's your board," Liz said behind me.

"Thanks." Absently I gripped the snowboard she slipped into my mitten. "I guess you heard all that."

"I guess everyone between here and Aspen

heard it," she murmured. "Why didn't you tell him you were sorry?"

"I—," I began. Truth was, I'd opened my mouth to apologize, since that was the logical thing to do after such a stupid mistake. But I'd still been so angry over something he hadn't really done, I couldn't get the words out.

So angry that I would have belittled what he loved or challenged him to a stupid contest if I'd had the chance.

"Nick Krieger," the crowd sighed, collectively recognizing Nick as he hopped onto the slope and sped toward the deck.

He dropped into the pipe and picked up incredible momentum down the side and across the flat, almost as if the pipe weren't filled with powder. The opposite wall launched him so high, I definitely would have lost my balance and rolled down the windows if I were him. Nick just grabbed his board in a method air, like it was nothing. He hung in the sky for an impossible second, then slid down the side.

"Oooh," said the crowd, followed a moment later by an "oooh" from the ski lodge.

He hit the same height in his next trick,

a 360. He couldn't do my tricks, but he went much higher, and he was so heavy and powerful that the pipe seemed to grind and bend underneath him. I could feel it in my teeth.

"Oooh," said the crowd.

He crossed the flat again and launched his third trick, a 540. I could tell the split second after he hit his apex that what he'd intended to do didn't match his rotation.

"That's not going to end well," Liz whispered as Nick headed for the snow without completing the last revolution. I'd seen a lot of crashes, courtesy of Josh and his peeps. I pictured this one in my head before it happened.

I couldn't watch. The snow in the air had thickened, but even so, I could see his dark silhouette headed downward. I closed my eyes.

"Biff!" yelled the crowd in unison.

I opened my eyes and gasped. "He's not moving."

Liz grabbed my padded arm.

I waited for Gavin and Davis to move from their places at the top of the course. A gray snow cloud of testosterone always hung over the half-pipe course, making boys try tricks they couldn't land and pretend not to be hurt when they were. Nick would be embarrassed if his friends went down to check on him. He would be horrified if I did. But *somebody* had to go. Nick got hit in football games all autumn long, and he was used to it. If he wasn't getting up, he was really hurt.

Finally, Gavin and Davis maneuvered their boards to the edge of the course and tipped over into the pipe, skidding to a stop just above Nick's dark, motionless body.

Through the thick snow, I saw him slowly rise.

I gasped again, and realized I'd been holding my breath.

He kicked off his snowboard and hoisted it behind his back to carry it home. The boarders around me on the lip of the course cheered for him.

"Thank God!" Liz exclaimed. "He can't be hurt too badly if he's walking away." She turned to me with her dark eyebrows raised in question. "Want to go after him?"

I did, desperately. I squinted through the snow after the dim retreating shapes of the three boys, Gavin and Davis sliding on their boards, Nick limping a little. "Better let him cool down first."

Liz puffed out a little sigh of relief. "Still want to get in that last run?"

"No. If it's okay with you, let's call it a night." I'd thought I wanted to squeeze every minute of boarding I could out of winter break. I'd never been the person to turn down one last run. And I should have been ecstatic that my snowboarding challenge with Nick was over now because he'd been injured.

But for once, my heart just wasn't in boarding. My heart was with Nick.

This was how my life worked: Something great happened simultaneously with something very bad. I won lessons with Daisy Delaney, but I had to snowboard off a cliff to get any benefit from them. I found the perfect pair of jeans, but they didn't belong to me, and they had BOY TOY written across the butt. Now my ugly bet with Nick had ended, so maybe we could finally get together. But oops—I had just screamed at him in front of a live audience, *and* he was probably crippled.

That night after supper I sat on my bed, staring at the cell phone in my hand. I'd already called Liz and Chloe. Both of them had promised to meet me on the slopes the next day just for fun, since the comp was obviously off after Nick's injury. More importantly, they said Davis and Gavin did not have an update on Nick's condition. Boys, it seemed, did not check on each other like girls.

Which was precisely my problem. I couldn't stand the thought of Nick hurting in his house without his mother home. Maybe his dad wasn't home, either. They might not even know he'd fallen. I had to make sure he was okay.

Nick had been angry enough at the half-pipe that he'd probably hang up on me when I called. Or worse, he'd be very polite, like he was at school to people he didn't know.

But his well-being was more important than my pride. I'd just entered his number from the school handbook into my cell phone. All I had to do was press the green button and the call would go through.

Good: I would find out whether Nick was okay.

Bad: Nick would view me as one of those girls at school who chased him, even after they'd gone on two dates and he'd called it quits.

Nick's number waited impatiently on the screen, tapping its foot. I could press the red button to cancel the call. Without pressing anything, I set the phone down on my bedside table, crossed my arms, and glared at it.

Good: Nick wouldn't think I was chasing him.

Bad: Nick would die alone in his house from complications related to his stupendous wipeout. The guilt of knowing I could have saved his life if not for my outsized ego would be too much for me to bear. I would retreat from public life. I would join a nearby convent and knit potholders from strands of my own hair. No, I would crochet Christmas ornaments in the shape of delicate snowflakes. Red snowflakes! They would be sold in the souvenir shops around town. I would support a whole orphanage from the proceeds of snowflakes I crocheted from my hair. All the townspeople of Snowfall would tell tourists the story of Crazy Sister Hayden and the tragedy of her lost love.

Or I could call Nick. Jesus! I snatched up

the phone and pressed the green button.

His phone switched straight to voice mail. Great, I hadn't found out whether he was dying, *and* if he recovered later, he would see my number on his phone and roll his eyes.

Damage control: *Beeeeep!* "Hey, Nick, it's Hayden. Just, ah, wanted to know how a crash like that feels." Wait, I was trying to get him to call me back, right? He would not return my call after a message like that. "Actually, just wondering whether you're ready to make out again and then have another argument." He might not return that call, either. "Actually, I remembered your mother isn't home, and I wanted to make sure you're okay. Please give me a call back."

Pressed red button. Set phone on nightstand. Folded arms. Glared at phone. Picked it up. "Freaking stupid young love!" I hollered, slamming it into the pillows on my bed. Doofus jumped up, startled.

Ah-ha.

I slipped into long underwear, layered on the BOY TOY jeans and shirts and sweaters and coats and hats, and waddled stiffly downstairs to find Doofus's leash. By now Josh and Mom were video-bowling. I hoped they were so absorbed that I could escape from the house just by calling a good-bye into the den as I passed the doorway.

But no. "Hayden," Mom called. "Where are you going all bundled up?"

"I'm taking Doofus for a walk," I said brightly.

"I already took Doofus for a walk," Josh said.

I stared at him. He stared right back at me while Mom took her turn bowling. I could have explained that I wanted to walk without Doofus and get some air. But it would be pretty unusual—one might even go so far as to say unheard of—for me to take a hike on a winter night when I was exhausted from boarding all day.

I could also come right out and tell both of them that Nick had fallen on the slopes today and I wanted to check on him. But then Mom would suggest I take the car to his house. And then I could never pull off the charade that I just happened by his mansion while walking my dog.

Besides, it was the principle of the thing— the very idea that Josh saw I wanted to walk Doofus and he was going out of his way to foil me, like a normal little brother. This made me angry. Did he *want* Nick to die on the floor of his bathroom from an overdose of mentholated rub? Did he *want* me to spend the last eighty years of my lifespan in a convent? Maybe he was mad that I was trying to sneak out of the house wearing his jeans for the third day in a row.

"I am taking Doofus for *another* walk," I said clearly, daring him to defy me.

"That would not be good for Doofus." Josh folded his arms. "Mom, that would not be good for Doofus."

Oh! Dragging Mom into this was low. Not to mention Doofus. "Since when is going for a walk not good for a dog?" I challenged Josh.

"He's an *old* dog!" Josh protested.

"He's *four*!" I pointed out.

"That's twenty-eight in dog years! He's practically thirty!"

"Strike!" Mom squealed amid the noise of electronic pins falling. Then she shook her game remote at both of us in turn. "I'm not stupid, you know. And I'm not as out of it as you assume. I know the two of you are really arguing about something else. It's those jeans again, isn't it?" She nodded to me. "I should cut them in half and give each of you a leg. Why does either of you want to wear jeans with 'boy toy' written across the seat anyway?"

"I thought that was the fashion," Josh said. "Grandma wears a pair of sweatpants with 'hot mama' written across the ass."

"That is *different*," Mom hissed. "She wears them around the *kitchen*."

I sniffed indignantly. "I *said*," I announced, "I am going for a walk with my dog. My beloved canine and I are taking a turn around our fair community. No activity could be more wholesome for a young girl and her pet. And if you have a problem with that, well! What is this world coming to? Come along, dear Doofus." I stuck my nose in the air and stalked past them, but the effect was lost. Somewhere around "our fair community," Mom and Josh both had lost interest and turned back to the TV.

Or so I thought. But just as I was about to step outside, Josh appeared in the doorway between the kitchen and the mud room. "What the hell are you doing?" he demanded.

I said self-righteously, "I am taking my loyal canine for a w—"

"You're going to Nick's, aren't you?" he

whispered. "Do you think that's a good idea? I heard you yelled at him for no reason at the half-pipe, right before he busted ass."

I swallowed. Good news traveled fast. "So?"

"So, why are you going over there? Best case scenario, you make out with him again and then have another fight."

Good news about *everything* traveled fast. I scowled at Josh. "It's better than not knowing whether he's hurt."

"Is it?" Josh leaned against the doorframe and folded his arms. He'd never looked so much like my father, and it was time to put him in his place.

"Way better, and someday you will be old enough to understand." I reached forward to pat him on the head. He dodged my hand and came after me across the mud room, bent on revenge. Doofus and I escaped out the door and ran all the way across the snowy yard. I wouldn't have put it past Josh to chase me outside in his socks, but behind me the mud room had turned dark.

Doofus and I headed toward town. The sidewalk was icy as always but not nearly as slippery, now that I wore good walking boots rather than snowboarding boots. And the night was gorgeous, deep purple all around with the lights of downtown glowing from the valley, and a sky full of stars. We skirted the touristy area, with its streets full of happy families and laughing couples in love, and headed up the mountain.

Nick's street was close to the center of town, but I couldn't recall ever driving up it in my mom's car. It allowed access to only ten mansions overlooking the slopes, the homes of nobody I knew except Nick. And somehow I had always resisted driving very slowly back and forth in front of his house. Willpower? No. I figured his front gate was equipped with security cameras and I would just be embarrassing myself. And this street was definitely not on the bus line.

Doofus and I hiked up the sidewalk. Since there was no one around, I dropped Doofus's leash. He pranced in the snowdrifts and bit the snow and rolled in it until ice clumped and froze in his tail. He promptly trotted back to me, wagging his tail, and whacked me with the ice.

"Ouch! Sweet doggie." We'd passed two mansions and had reached Nick's. It was big and beautiful and distant amid the snow falling gently in the night. Through the cold landscape, warm light glowed from a second-story window. If he'd died alone in his big, empty house, at least he hadn't died in the cold dark.

I couldn't leave without knowing. With a sigh, I pressed the button on the imposing gate. Doofus and I both jumped at the buzz. I backed up to give the gate room in case it opened out.

It stayed shut.

After a few moments, I pressed the button again. The gate didn't move, and the lights of the house stared at me across the snowy plain.

"Fine. Come on, Doofus." I led the way back down the hill to the narrow passage between the Kriegers' fence and the fence next door. Mistake: The unshoveled snow was knee-deep. I kept right on wading through it. "This is because I'm a good person," I assured Doofus. "I am going to heaven, though hopefully not by way of the convent." Doofus pranced happily around me.

Finally I reached the back corner of Nick's enormous yard, where even the passage between the Kriegers' fence and their neighbors' was shut off from the ski slopes by another, higher fence. "Okay, this isn't good. I'm sorry, Doofus, but I have to leave you out here while I go save the day. I'll only be a minute." I looked around for a tree to tie Doofus's leash to, one that he would not pull out by its roots.

Something moved swiftly in the corner of my eye. Mountain lion! I gasped and whirled around.

It was only Doofus, climbing Nick's fence. He'd leapt to the top and hooked his front paws over the wood. Now his back legs scrabbled against the smooth planks, searching for a claw-hold to push him over.

"Bad dog," I sighed. He'd disappeared.

Well, if I'd had any thoughts of chickening out on my mission, they were gone now. I jumped to the top of the fence, hauled myself over, and dropped to the snowy ground.

And froze with horror. The mountain lion was *here* in the fenced yard with us where we couldn't escape. *Growling* at us. Except for the square rectangular glow of a glass door on the deck, I saw nothing but blackness. But I heard the growl, too close.

"Doofus!" I screamed, needlessly. He barreled toward me and hit me in the chest, yelping. I'm not sure whether I dragged him or he dragged me, but somehow we dashed up the wooden steps to the snow-covered deck and headed straight for the door. I didn't even have time to pray it was unlocked. The sharp claws of the mountain lion nicked my calves above my boots, through my long underwear and jeans. I yanked open the door and picked Doofus up bodily. We collapsed inside in a mound of Polartec and fur and backed against the door until it clicked closed.

We both started away from the door as the mountain lion leaped against it, howling, all fangs and claws and wild eyes.

Very small wild eyes. Four of them.

It wasn't a mountain lion at all. It was two tabbies.

There were a few seconds of stillness, just Doofus and me panting in the large, quiet room, and bemusement that I had exploded with my wet dog into a filthy-rich family's grand home. We faced a huge rock fireplace that I recognized from the Krieger Meats and Meat Products TV commercial so many years ago, with Nick giving the camera his winning smile, his mother blinking pleasantly into the camera, and Mr. Krieger inviting the public to taste Krieger Meats, from their family to yours. Happier times for Nick and his parents.

Feeling a pang for all of them, I gave Doofus's wet, cold fur a stroke. I wasn't sure what to do now. I still needed to find out whether Nick was okay. And there were still attack cats on the prowl.

I was about to detangle myself from Doofus and survey the damage we'd done to Nick's palace when I caught another movement out of the corner of my eye. Someone was lying on a leather couch facing away from me. A blond head eased ominously into view. Nick's father! Oh, no! He would take me for a stalker. Now Nick would *really* think I was chasing him!

Or not. Mr. Krieger took out one earbud. He cackled in a high-pitched witch voice, "I'll get you, my pretty, and your little dog Toto, too!"

"Uh, Doofus," I corrected him.

He pursed his lips quizzically. "Come on. It wasn't *that* bad a joke."

I didn't bother to explain. I wouldn't need to get along with Mr. Krieger in the future. Something told me I would never find myself eating Thanksgiving dinner with these people—and wait until the owner of Krieger Meats and Meat Products found out I was a vegetarian! I just wanted to satisfy myself that Nick was okay, and then get out. "Hi, there!" I beamed. "Did you order a redhead and a dog?"

"Hayden O'Malley," he purred.

"Yes, sir." He knew who I was? Doofus was licking my face.

Mr. Krieger pulled out his other earbud. "I know all about your challenge with Nick. My money's on you, literally. Nick's a quitter."

I blinked at him, not sure what to say to that. I'd never heard a parent say something so mean about his child—and something so untrue. I reminded myself that his wife had left him the previous weekend, and he was probably not in the best of moods. If Nick had hidden his injury from his dad and hadn't yet told him the challenge was over, I didn't want to be the one to clue his dad in and mess things up worse for Nick. I said carefully, "Yeah, the girls at school are always pushing him down on the playground and telling him not to be such a baby."

Mr. Krieger sat up straighter on the couch and glared at me. Great. I was definitely not getting invited for Thanksgiving now. At least I'd made my point, and I thought he'd heard me.

"Is he in?" I prompted Mr. Krieger.

He swept his hand dramatically toward a wide staircase, then reinserted his earbuds and sank back onto the couch, dismissing me. I supposed this meant I was invited in? Or at least, not thrown out? Doofus and I righted ourselves and walked past the couch and up the stairs. Doofus's claws clicked on the stone and echoed against the vaulted ceilings.

On the second story, windows overlooking the ski slopes lined one side of the vast hallway. The other side was an endless stretch of doors. I headed toward the open door with light flooding out onto the Navajo rug. But I stopped short when I heard Nick talking inside. There was a pause, and then he talked again. He must be on the phone, which is why my own call had gone straight to his voice mail.

"I love you, too," I heard him say. "'Bye."

My heart stopped. Had he been on the phone with Fiona? Or some new snow bunny I hadn't yet heard about? Whoever his new girlfriend was . . . it wasn't me.

shred

(shred) *v.* **1.** to tear up the slopes **2.** or Hayden's heart

Before I could react, he called, "Come in."

I froze like a rabbit, just as I had outside the men's locker room at the health club yesterday. This time Nick really *had* caught me.

I couldn't very well run away. Mr. Krieger knew I was there. Finally, I sauntered forward and lounged in the doorway with my arms crossed on my chest. After all, *I'd* caught *Nick* telling someone he loved her. Someone other than me.

He lay with his legs on his king-size bed and his body folded forward off the edge, toward the floor, in what looked suspiciously like a cockamamy approximation of a Downward-Facing Dog. The football players in the huge posters all around the room seemed to rush toward him, taunting him, while he lay helpless in the center of the circle and tried in vain to stretch his back.

I'd discovered so many new sides of Nick in the past few days, and now I was seeing another. His dark hair had been long the whole time I'd known him. I'd never glimpsed the nape of his neck, but here it was, bare to me as his hair touched the floor. Doofus sauntered over and licked Nick's face. Squinting against the dog slobber, Nick grumbled, "You may be a lot of things, Hayden, but quiet isn't one of them."

I sniffed. "Oh, yeah? You weren't very quiet on the phone just now, either."

He eyed me. Even from his upside-down viewpoint, he must have been able to see I was jealous. "That was my mom," he explained.

My heart started beating again, painfully. I kept my face carefully neutral, hiding how freaking relieved I felt that he hadn't given up on us and moved along to another girl. Not yet, anyway.

"She's staying with my grandmother in Phoenix." Nick sat up on his bed with a groan, looking hurt and adorable in a tight T-shirt and track pants, his hair a disaster. "What are you doing here?"

"I just happened to be in the neighborhood, walking my dog . . ." This was sounding lame. ". . . several miles from my home, in the middle of the night, in the snow. And I found myself in your backyard."

His eyes flew wide open. "With the cats?"

"If that's what you call them."

"You came over because you feel guilty for yelling at me at the half-pipe."

I did. He didn't have to sound so smug about it, though. "I do feel sort of guilty for yelling at you at the half-pipe," I admitted, "but—"

"But—," he broke in sarcastically.

"But," I continued over him, "I've had good reason in the past to think you'd called me a name like that to your friends."

"What's your good reason? That I *didn't* call you a fire-crotch last week in the lunchroom?"

He had me there, but I wasn't ready to admit defeat. Nick was just as guilty as I was. "You're one to talk. You walked around mad at me for something *I* didn't mean to do for a whole day, until I persuaded you otherwise."

"And then *I* apologized," he pointed out. One side of his mouth cocked up in a mischievous grin. "And then I slipped you the tongue."

We both cracked up then, with spontaneous exclamations of "The tongue!" I was glad we'd broken the ice. At the same time, it seemed like we were laughing about a relationship we'd had long ago, rather than last night. Maybe we had nothing in common now that the bet was off.

I hoped not. To show him that a sequel to "the tongue" was not out of the question, I crossed his room, shedding layers of outerwear as I went, and sat beside him on the bed. "Seriously, I came over to make sure you're okay. Did you go to the doctor?"

"I'm not hurt," he said flatly.

I rolled my eyes in exasperation. "I was there this afternoon, Nick. I saw you fall. You were lying immobile in the snow."

"Yeah. I didn't get enough—"

"—rotation in the 540," we said simultaneously.

We paused, watching each other. All our problems fell away. Just for a moment we were friends, fellow snowboarders, discussing a mistake we'd both made a million times. This was not my imagination. Nick felt it, too. He looked deep into my eyes. His own eyes were impossibly dark with the lights of his room reflecting as little halos.

And then he looked away, flicking his hair out of his face with his pinkie. "So anyway, after I busted ass, I'm lying there in the snow. My life flashed before my eyes."

"Why?" I asked, horrified, scooting closer.

"Not my whole life, I guess. My personal life. I've been kind of down about my parents, and I was mad at you for yelling at me, and then I wondered why we're doing this stupid comp anyway. Gavin's been breathing down my neck about winning him Poser tickets and putting Chloe in her place. All I ever wanted to do this winter break was have fun and board and relax."

"Amen," I sighed. Thank God the comp was over. "I was worried about you. I called your cell and rang the bell at the gate. You didn't hear it?"

"It rings downstairs, and my dad . . ." Nick stared into space, and his voice trailed off.

I could have finished this sentence for him. *My dad . . . is lying on the couch, listening to the middle-aged person's equivalent of emo songs on his iPod, because my mother left him.* Journey, or something. Duran Duran.

Finally Nick focused on me again. His long, dark lashes blinked slowly. He looked lost. A more accurate end to his sentence: *My dad . . . is lost himself, and I don't know whether my parents are coming back.*

I wanted to reach out to him then, to touch his stubbled cheek with my fingertips. We were alone in his bedroom, after all. On his bed. His mom was gone. His dad probably didn't care what we did. Doofus stretched into a different position on Nick's carpet, sending a wave of wet dog odor toward us only occasionally. We could have made out.

But maybe Josh actually had a point, and it wasn't good for Nick and me to keep making out and arguing. Perhaps making out was *not* the answer to all our problems, oddly enough. And I'd come over to check on Nick, not to seduce him. Shaking my head to clear it, I said, "I know what will make you feel better."

"I'm not hurt," he insisted.

"Obviously you are, or I wouldn't have walked in on you doing half-assed yoga." I stretched out on his bed and hung forward over the side, just as I'd found him. "Come on, I'll do it with you."

Grumbling, Nick bent over the side with me. We hung that way for about ten seconds of quiet before he said, "It's not working."

"That's your problem, like I told you yesterday. You don't hold the stretch long enough, and besides, you do it while listening to"—I felt behind me on the bed for his MP3 player and peered at the screen—"alt metal." I tossed it across the room into a leather armchair. "Try this with me. Inhale through your nose, and let your legs melt into the bed. Exhale through your mouth, and let your body and your arms fall toward the floor." I led him through a few more long breaths that way, until I could see from the corner of my eye that he'd relaxed, like when we'd made out last night.

I reminded myself yet again that this was not the time for making out. I was making up with Nick for exploding at him in public about the fire-crotch comment. As he stretched with his eyes closed, he looked so young and vulnerable, so *normal*, that I ached to reach out and feel around on his back for the bruise where he'd fallen, or to change my voice from soothing to sexy. But I'd come here on a mission to make Nick feel better. And I was pretty sure making out with me was not what Nick needed right now. I took him through a whole series of easy poses, moving from the bed to the floor.

Finally we sat up. Nick slouched glassy-eyed against his leather armchair. I relaxed in the Lotus Pose, invigorated from the stretches.

"I feel better," he said languidly.

"I'm glad."

"No, really better," he said like he couldn't believe it now that he was waking up a little.

"Keep stretching every day and take it seriously, and you won't be as likely to get hurt boarding. Now I'd better go." I nodded at the clock on his bedside table. "I told my mom I was taking Doofus for a walk. We could have walked to Leadville by now."

He stood up unsteadily, leaning on the chair. "I'll drive you home."

I wasn't sure this was a good idea. I had

a lot of anxiety about him being polite to me. It would probably be best to give him more time to cool off after I'd yelled at him at the half-pipe.

On the other hand, I *really* did not want to walk back home through the freezing night or make Doofus do it, either. He'd been through enough. "Is your SUV parked outside, or is it in the garage?" I asked hopefully. "Doofus and I would rather not face your attack cats again."

"There's a cat door in the back of the house. They can come inside any time they want. Don't worry. I'll protect you." He slid a machine gun from his dresser—a red-and-blue plastic water gun.

"My hero," I breathed as he pointed his gun into the hall and looked both ways before stealthily motioning for me and Doofus to follow, like he was the star of an action-adventure flick. With me giggling at him and him shushing me as if I really were his airheaded heroine, we made it downstairs and stepped from an enormous, gleaming kitchen into a three-car garage.

His SUV, so familiar to me from seeing it parked every day at school since he'd gotten his license last year, looked out of place in the vast space next to a Porsche. The SUV seemed so . . . normal. Like Nick: normal but not. He didn't mind an Irish setter dripping melted snow on his bedroom carpet or hopping into the back of his SUV. Yet his SUV was parked in the garage of a mansion.

You know what else was perfectly normal? The missing third car. His parents had separated, just like Liz's parents had divorced three years before. The Krieger Meats and Meat Products fortune did not solve everything. I tried not to stare back at the empty space on the other side of the Porsche as the garage door tipped out of the way and the SUV pulled into the light snow.

Snowflakes zoomed around in the headlight beams, defining them far out in front of us, almost all the way down the hill to the gate. Nick turned on the windshield wipers, but he hardly needed them. The snowflakes weren't substantial. The breeze of the wipers shooed them away like fireflies during a Tennessee summer.

He pushed another button, and the gate majestically opened for us before we even reached it. He didn't mean anything by this motion, I reminded myself. He drove through the gate a few times a day. He didn't give it a second thought. He had no idea that, to me, he seemed to be rubbing in how rich he was and how powerful his parents were. This was what had separated us in the seventh grade, when he'd half-believed Gavin that a girl wouldn't date him without his family status behind him. This was what separated us still.

And yet, in a strange way, I'd never felt closer to him. The SUV crunched through gravel onto the main road, where it swished through slushy snow. But inside it was warm, and a rock ballad from the Poser CD whispered about true love lost. This should have been a date. Instead of him taking me home after I came to check on him and got run inside by killer cats, he should have been taking me back to my house after we'd watched a movie together at his. He would come inside. My parents would go to bed, and Josh would take a hint and abandon video-bowling to go upstairs and read a book. (I could dream, couldn't I?) Nick and I would be alone with the smoldering embers of a fire. And then we would—

"—get out?" he was asking me.

I blinked at him across the dark SUV.

"I beg your pardon?" I hoped to God I hadn't been discussing any of this out loud.

"Are. You. Going. To. Get. Out?" he asked more distinctly. We'd already parked in front of my house, with the SUV's heater still bathing us in warmth against the snowy night outside. "You haven't said a word the whole five-minute drive here. Are you sick?" He reached across the cab and put his hot hand on my forehead.

I laughed and pulled his hand down. But I didn't let it go. I kept it there in both my hands, on my knee. And he didn't pull it away. We watched each other for a quiet moment.

"I'm glad this happened," he said softly.

He was so handsome in the soft and snowy moonlight. I wanted him to be talking about our relationship: He was glad we'd finally gotten together. But after everything that had passed between us this week, doubts still lurked at the back of my mind about whether he seriously liked me, or he intended to date me twice and dump me like all his other girlfriends, or the whole thing was just a joke to him. I hoped it was for real, and I didn't want to talk about it too much and ruin the lovely illusion that we were a couple. So I said noncommittally, "Me too."

"Because I've been trying to get you back since the seventh grade."

I must have given him a very skeptical look.

He laughed at my expression. "Yeah, I have a funny way of showing it. I know. But you're always on my mind. You're in the front of my mind, on the tip of my tongue. So if someone breaks a beaker in chemistry class, I raise my hand and tell Ms. Abernathy you did it. If somebody brings a copy of *Playboy* to class, I stuff it in your locker."

"Oh!" I thought back to the January issue. "I wondered where that came from."

"And if Everett Walsh tells the lunch table what a wicked kisser you are and how far he would have gotten with you if his mother hadn't come in——"

I stamped my foot on the floorboard of the SUV. "That is so not true! He'd already gotten as far as he was going. He's not *that* cute, and I had to go home and study for algebra."

"——it drives me insane to the point that I tell him to shut up or I'll make him shut up right there in front of everybody. Because *I* am supposed to be your boyfriend, and *my* mother is supposed to hate you, and you're supposed to be making out with *me*."

Twisted as this declaration was, it was the sweetest thing a boy had ever said to me. I dwelled on the soft lips that had formed the statement, and on the meaning of his words. "Okay." I scooted across the seat and nibbled the very edge of his superhero chin.

"Ah," he gasped, moving both hands from the steering wheel to the seat to brace himself. "I didn't mean *now*. I meant in general. Your dad will come out of your house and kill me."

"He won't," I murmured against Nick's neck. "He came home while I was gone and went to bed early because he's so pooped." I glanced at my watch to make sure. "Yeah. He teaches four Pilates classes on Thursdays." Then, just to be mean, I did a real number on Nick's neck, like I would want *him* to move his mouth on *my* neck. I had to be careful or I would give him a hickey. Served him right for playing hard to get.

"Damn it," he grunted in frustration. He put his hand in my hair and pulled my head back. Our eyes met for a second. I saw how frustrated he was, and how hot for me, and something else between his dark brows.

And then *he* kissed *me*. His mouth was on mine, covering mine and making me feel small. His tongue swept inside. He pulled my nape with his big hand to adjust me to exactly where he wanted me. The air in the SUV flashed too hot and then cold as he kissed me. His other hand slid up my thigh.

I would never have admitted this to anyone, and I would only put up with it for so long. But this was the part of a relationship with Nick I'd dreamed about and longed for: Nick in control of me.

He murmured against *my* neck, "See? We can't do this in an SUV on your street in the open." His tone was triumphant, as if he'd conquered me. *Yeah!*

"You win," I sighed. Then I opened my eyes.

He gazed down at me, wearing the most beautiful smile. Nick Krieger was not putting on a brave face for the public. He was not faking. He was genuinely happy.

With me!

And then, it turned out that *I* won, because I got what I wanted. He kissed me for several long minutes.

Finally, he slid his hand from my nape down to my shoulder and squeezed there for a second, catching his breath. "Come on. I'll walk you to the door." Before I could argue about that (after all, who *really* wants a gentleman for a boyfriend, besides Liz?), he walked around the SUV and opened the hatchback to let out Doofus, whom I had forgotten about completely.

I resented Doofus a little. First he'd jumped into my arms when the cats attacked and made me smell like dog. Now, if it weren't for him, I could have hung around oustide, chatting Nick up until he agreed to get back in the SUV and make out with me for a few more minutes. As it was, Doofus would be tugging on his leash the whole time and trying to pull my arm out of its socket.

To my surprise, as I watched in the rearview mirror, Doofus leaped out of the SUV, dragging his leash. I tensed, prepared to lunge from the SUV after him. I pictured chasing him all over the neighborhood. I'd had enough snowy walks for one night, not to mention snowy runs to escape death at the paws of wild animals.

Fortunately, he didn't run away from my

house. He ran toward it. He must have been hungry. He ran straight for the fence—at this point, I suspected brain damage from our fall through the Kriegers' back door—and hooked his paws over the top of the fence, just as he had at Nick's house. He scrabbled with his back paws until his big red dog-booty disappeared over the fence.

If he could come and go over the fence as he pleased, there was no telling what he did all around the neighborhood while we weren't watching. Suddenly, it seemed the O'Malleys were having a hard time keeping track of their dog *and* their daughter.

Nick seemed to be thinking the same thing as he opened the passenger door for me. "Did you see that?"

"Yep," I laughed, swinging his hand as we walked across the snowy lawn toward the mud room door.

"This *is* your house, right?"

"Either that, or some naked hot-tubbers behind that fence just got the surprise of their lives." We'd reached the door. I leaned back against it, looking way up at him, thinking the strangest thoughts, such as, *Nick Krieger is finally my boyfriend!*

"I'm boarding with Liz and Chloe tomorrow," I said. "Maybe I could come over to your house again afterward and check on you?" I raised my eyebrows to *hint hint* what I meant by *checking on him*. With any luck, his father would be as uninvolved and dismissive as he'd been tonight. Nick needed more yoga in his bedroom, and possibly a physical.

"I'm boarding, too," he said, "but that doesn't mean you can't check on me afterward." He raised his eyebrows too, *hint hint*.

It wasn't funny when he did it. "What do you mean, you're boarding?" I asked suspiciously. "You're hurt."

"I keep telling you, I'm not hurt that badly. It's no worse than a football hit, and I get those all the time and keep playing. I have to beat you in a comp in two days."

I put my hands on my hips and looked up at him. "The comp is canceled because you're injured!"

He shook his head stubbornly. "I'm not injured. The comp is not canceled. Everybody in town knows about our bet. I can't quit now. My dad would kill me. My dad has actually bet *against* me. Winners never quit."

Exasperated, I ran my hands through my hair. "Nick, I understand you want to impress your dad, but it's not worth risking your health."

"My he—" he began. Then he took a step backward into the snow, and his broad shoulders sagged in defeat. "That's the only reason you came over, isn't it? Just like going outside with me last night. You want me to call off the comp because you're so scared of that jump."

I hadn't even thought of the jump all night. I'd thought only of Nick. Now those fears flooded back to me, paired with his unfair accusation. I nearly started crying right there against the mud room door. But I managed to say "No" while looking into his eyes. "I am not a liar."

We glared at each other in the starlight, clouds of our frozen breath mingling in the space between us. I realized then that the pain of crushing on him would continue for the whole year and a half of high school I had left. We would not get together, no matter how hard Chloe and Liz wished it. We couldn't. Try as we might, Nick and I could not find a way to graduate from the seventh grade.

"Whatever." Stomping through the snow toward his SUV, he called over his shoulder,

"See you at the comp on Saturday. And by the way"—he opened the door and slid inside—"I did get your message about making out and then having an argument. I guess you got what you wanted. Now don't call me again." He slammed the door. Snow bounced off the hood from the shock wave. He cranked the engine and drove away down my street. Even after he'd turned the corner and disappeared, the strains of the Poser love song still reached me in the quiet snowy night.

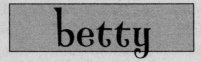

(be′ tē) *n.* **1.** a girl who isn't used to snowboarding and is liable to have a fatal accident any second **2.** Chloe

I dragged myself downstairs the next morning, hardly excited about boarding with Liz and Chloe. The sitch with Nick, or lack thereof, was so depressing.

Mom and Dad busied themselves with breakfast so they could get out the door and head for Boulder, where they would be spending the night. Personally, I wouldn't have picked Friday the thirteenth for my date night. But tomorrow night, the real Valentine's Day, they'd be running Parents'

Night Out for members of the health club. In years past, they'd made me work Parents' Night Out with them. This year they'd let me off babysitting because they figured I might have fancy teenage Valentine's Day plans, maybe even a Poser concert. If only they knew.

Josh watched me as I walked in and sat down. Then he watched the TV on the counter for a few seconds. Then he looked straight at me. I stuck out my tongue at him. He looked at the TV, then widened his eyes at me. Finally I got it. I turned to see what on TV could possibly be so important.

Me. Snowboarding! The local access channel cycled through the same few items over and over: birthday announcements, club meetings, a recording of the latest city council meeting, a film of Everett Walsh leading the high school Scholars' Bowl to annihilate Telluride. Now the channel listed the scores from the Snowfall Amateur Challenge in front of footage of me in the half-pipe. Hey, nice form.

My mom headed toward me with a plate of oatmeal and fruit—tripped over Doofus—and managed not to spill anything. Athleticism obviously ran in the family. She sat down and followed my gaze to the TV. "Hayden, your dad and I heard you have some kind of snowboarding bet with your boyfriend, Nick."

I choked on a strawberry and glared at Josh, who shrugged. He hadn't ratted on me. So I told my mom, "Nick is not my boyfriend. He may have charmed you at the health club the other day, and we did indeed both go to Mile-High Pie afterward, but we were not there *together*." At least, not at first. "Don't adults have adult bets to gossip about?"

"Are you kidding?" my dad asked—tripping over Doofus—and sitting down at his place with his breakfast intact on his plate. Good save. "He was your little friend when we first moved here, right? It's a battle of the exes. Bets about golf aren't nearly that juicy."

Mom went on, "Word on the street—"

Josh snorted.

"—is that you won't win because of your fear of heights. Now, with your lessons with Daisy Delaney coming up soon, haven't you changed your mind? Don't you want me to make an appointment for you with a doctor who can help you get over your phobia?"

"Yes," said Josh.

"No!" I shouted. I ignored the three of them eyeing one another over my outburst. Me, I eyed my image on TV, landing a 900 like it was nothing. Nick was right. I was chicken, and it was now or never.

"So think back to that moment," Chloe coaxed me, "when your mom was offering you help. Picture her face when you go off this jump all by yourself."

"Yeah, it was weird that she mentioned the bet this morning," I said flatly. "If I didn't know she had to work Valentine's night, I'd say she had a bet for Poser tickets herself. No pressure." After eight hours on the slopes, the last two at the jump, I was getting a little tired of Chloe's motivational speeches.

Liz must have sensed I was about to blow. She nudged the tips of her skis between my board and Chloe's in the snow. "Let's review the progress we *have* made today. We've done the boardercross, and though we're not sure Hayden can beat Nick there, we're satisfied she's going as fast as she can go."

"Unless I eat a lot of meats and meat products to gain weight between now and tomorrow morning," I interjected.

"Yuck," Liz said at the same time as Chloe put her glove on my cheek and turned my head to face her. "Focus!"

"We've done the half-pipe," Liz continued, "and we're confident Hayden will kick Nick's butt there."

"Yes, but only if we employ careful strategy, as in rock-paper-scissors," I said. "My 720 totally beats Nick falling down, like paper covers rock. Unless the rock is a boy, in which case the boy always wins."

"Hayden—" Liz began.

"I am getting sick of your attitude, Hayden," Chloe talked over Liz. "We've been up here all day with you. All we have left is to get you off this jump. Every time you try, you have some excuse: wind in your face, bug in your ear, panties up your butt—"

"I was not making that up," I broke in. "Imagine trying a trick with uncomfortable underwear." I squirmed, rocking back and forth on my board to make my point.

"Or you make some stupid joke!" Chloe hollered at me. Her voice echoed against the rocky slope of the mountain overhead.

I stealthily looked around in my goggles to see if any boarders I knew had heard, but it was getting late, and the slopes were empty except for us.

"I'm beginning to think you don't *want* to get over your fear of heights," she said.

Suddenly, the mountain was quiet, except for the wind swishing through the tree branches and swaying their loads of snow. A few storm clouds approached from over the next peak. "I *do* want to get over my fear of heights," I said.

"You don't," Chloe insisted. "You're in your comfort zone. As long as everything stays right here, exactly the same, you can handle it. Guess what, Hayden? If you stay right here without ever trying anything new, you know where you'll be ten years from now?"

"In a convent?" I guessed.

"I seriously doubt *that*," Liz said.

"Right here." Chloe grabbed one of Liz's ski poles and planted it in the snow. "Here. In Snowfall. Still trying to go off this jump. Not at the X Games. Not at the Olympics. Here."

"I like it here," I whispered.

"Obviously," Chloe said.

"Let's end this on a high note," Liz suggested. "Chloe, why don't you tell her about the surprise?"

I rolled my eyes. "Did you set me and Nick up so we can make out and then have a huge fight?"

"Better!" Chloe jerked her head and arms wide in a dramatic flourish. A few rhinestones from her goggles went flying, lost forever, white against white in the deep snow. "Remember how I promised to get three unbiased judges for the comp? And remember how I couldn't board with you yesterday because I had something to take care of?"

"You didn't," I breathed.

"I did! I got Daisy Delaney to come over from Aspen, *and* her boyfriend, who's also a pro. That way the boys can't say you won just because the girl voted for the girl. All I had to do was give her and her boyfriend a complimentary night at the hotel. Though it probably didn't hurt that I also gave her some background on your challenge with your ex." She wagged her eyebrows at me, making her goggles move up and down. The bling remaining around the rim glittered in the sun. "One of the resort's snowboard instructors gladly offered to serve as the third judge when I told him Daisy Delaney was coming. The resort photographer may be there to capture the event on film. And—oh yeah—the newspaper."

"Isn't this great?" Liz prompted me gently, patting my padded arm.

"No pressure," I growled.

"Honestly, you need to get used to it," Liz said ominously. "A professional snowboarding career is nothing but pressure."

"Honestly," I yelled so loudly that she released my arm in surprise, "the two of you are not helping!" I turned on Chloe. "Didn't you advise me to take control? Well, how am I supposed to do that if the two of you manipulate every facet of my life?"

"Another excuse," Chloe declared. "I can't *believe* you made me *snowboard* today for this. My cheeks are chapped, and for what? Come on, Liz." Under her wooly rainbow hat, her blond ponytail flipped around, dissing me, as she boarded away.

I turned to Liz. "Well? What are you waiting for? Go on, Liz."

Liz reached out to pluck her ski pole from where Chloe had poked it into the snow. "I think you're just tired," she said gently.

"How could I be tired? I haven't done anything. That's the whole problem." Actually,

I was bone-tired, just as I'd felt a few times this week when Nick had made me feel bad about myself. I hadn't gone off the jump, but *thinking* about going off the jump and gathering all my energy only to pull out at the last second had totally drained me.

And then I started to cry.

"I'm sorry, Hayden," Liz said instantly. "I shouldn't have let Chloe pick those judges." She skied over to hug me.

"No, I'm sorry," I sobbed. "I'm making everybody mad at each other and now at me, and for what? For nothing!"

"It's not for nothing," Liz said soothingly. "Let's ask the boys for an extension. We'll do the comp on Sunday instead of tomorrow. Daisy won't care that she missed it, since she'll get a free hotel room anyway. Chloe and I will come back to the mountain with you tomorrow and work with you until you go off the jump. We'll figure something out."

"The Poser concert is tomorrow night, so Sunday will be too late for the bet," I cried. "Plus, the boys would never let us do that. They want me to fail anyway, so why would they give me another chance to succeed? Plus, it would just be an extra day for me to screw up, and to lose one more friend. Let's face it, I'm done." My goggles had fogged up inside with my tears. I tore them off, along with my hat. The wind was shockingly cold on my bare, wet face. "Totally useless, totally done."

"Hayden!" Chloe screamed from somewhere downhill.

Liz and I glanced at each other for only a second, then whipped around in a rush of powder. Chloe had been headed to the pass through the trees onto Main Street. I feared the worst, and I knew Liz did, too. People around here only half-laughed at Sonny Bono jokes. Skiers and boarders were killed every year running into trees, not just betties like Chloe but also experienced boarders. I slid across the snow as fast as I could, throwing all my weight into it. I stopped sideways at the edge of the stand of trees and sent a wave of snow arcing into the dark trunks.

Chloe was in the trees all right, way down the slope from us. I picked out her pink clothes right away against the white. She must have hit a mogul in the snowy path and veered into the trees. She was sitting upright, though, and none of her limbs pointed the wrong way. Ugh ugh ugh, I shrugged off that thought and called to her. "Are you okay?"

"Okay," she called back. "Just stuck. My board's buried and kind of pinned against this tree and my boot won't come loose. Aren't your boots supposed to pop out of your bindings when you suffer a major biff?"

This was not the time to point out to Chloe that her "major biff" was likely a low-speed slide of ultrabetty-ness. And if she hadn't been able to free her boots by now, I wouldn't be able to talk her through it. I would have to show her.

"Hold on," I called, popping off my board. The snow between the trees was piled up much higher than the snow on the slopes, which the sun melted and skiers wore down all day. There was no telling what lurked underneath the snow in the woods. Most likely, it wasn't safe to board across. Boarding boots weren't the safest footwear for hiking, either, but I couldn't leave Chloe. Darkness was falling.

"You want me to go with you?" Liz asked, stopping on her skis behind me.

"Nah, but bring my board if I'm able to haul her out the other side. And see if you can find my goggles and my hat. I dropped them somewhere." I put one boot into the soft snow at the very edge of the slope and sank much farther than I'd imagined, up to my hip.

"Watch that first step," Liz called.

I didn't even retort, I was so focused on Chloe downhill from me. Every step I took was deeper than the last, and it grew harder to bring my other foot around. Once I sank into a snowdrift all the way to the ground and slipped on the rocks underneath, like disappearing under the surface of a frozen lake.

"Hayden, are you still there?" Chloe screamed.

"I'm still here." At least, I thought I was. The daylight vanished even more quickly here under the bare trees, and the white all around disoriented me.

"Do you want me to call the boys?" Liz suggested from way above me.

"Do *not* call Nick Krieger!" I shouted. "God, would he love this."

"I've got Davis in my cell phone," Liz called. "Gavin, too."

"Absolutely not. If you call Davis *or* Gavin, Nick will be attached."

Chloe squealed, "Yes, please, Liz. Gavin would be excellent right now! No offense, Hayden, but don't join the ski patrol anytime soon."

"Ingrate!" I yelled. "I'll show you. I'm about to save the day, in just a minute here." I'd reached a patch where the snow was shallower, only knee-deep again. I seemed to be on an outcropping of rock, because my boots slid around beneath me worse than ever. Luckily, I'd almost reached Chloe. She was ten yards downhill from me.

"Tick-tock," she said. Through the low-hanging branches between us, I could see her haughty expression, like she was *still angry* with me.

Now *I* was mad. Even though they were water-resistant, my boarding clothes weren't meant to be immersed in snow. I was freezing. I expected at least a *little* gratitude from this diva. "Apologize for what you said to me at the jump," I demanded.

"Never!" she cried, sitting up straighter in her snowdrift.

"You are really testing me, Chloe," I muttered as I took one tentative step into even lighter snow cover. Now I could actually see the icy rocks underneath. "I am trying pretty hard to remember how nice you were to me that night with Nick in seventh graaaaade!" My boot slipped out from under me and I skidded straight into the claw-like branches in front of me. I managed to turn my head in time to avoid getting an eye poked out, and I waited until my body stopped and settled against the springy branches.

"Oh God!" Chloe squealed. "Are you okay?"

"Yep." I thought so. My face stung, and the thought crossed my mind that I was scarred for life. But I was sure the pain came from skidding across the snow on my cheek, not from a branch cutting me. I had a hard time extricating myself from the tree, though, and my head was getting cold. Finally, slowly, I rose up to kneel in the snow and asked Chloe, "Am I all in one piece?"

Her eyes flew wide open. I knew it was *really* bad when she almost screamed, but she slapped her hand over her mouth in time. She said, too calmly, "Hayden, put pressure on your ear."

"Put pressure on my ear," I puzzled out. "Why?" I touched my ear. It was wet, but so was the rest of me by now. Then I looked at my mitten. It glistened with blood.

"Call Josh," I whispered before I passed out.

"Hayden, that's going to take one stitch." Thank God for Josh. He sounded far off, even though I could feel his hands on my face. I couldn't quite make my way back to consciousness. Not while stitches were the topic of conversation.

"She's too heavy for me to carry," Josh said.

I tried to insult him back, but I didn't make a sound.

"Should I call the ski patrol?" Liz asked.

"No, they'll make a huge deal, and our parents will wig out and come home. They're over in Boulder for their first night out of town alone in a year. This is no biggie. She did the same thing when she gashed her arm at the skateboard park last summer. We just need to get her down the mountain. Call Nick."

"No!" I tried to exclaim but didn't. Wait—if Chloe was still lodged against the tree, dying of hypothermia, did it really matter who got called? Any hero would do.

"Hayden," said Nick.

My cheeks tingled with cold, and when I opened my eyes, all I saw was a blue glow. I must have face-planted. "Get Chloe," I told the snow. "She's stuck."

"Gavin and Davis have her." Nick's hands were on my shoulder and my waist. He rolled me onto my back. Now my wet face froze all over again in the cold wind. I opened my eyes.

Even though he was kneeling beside me in the snow, he towered above me like a movie superhero. Beyond his strong shoulders and the snowy trees, the sky glowed orange, and a few low clouds sugared him with snow. As I watched, he unzipped and pulled off his parka, then unbuttoned and tossed off his flannel shirt. He pulled his T-shirt over his head and shook his hair out of his eyes. Leaning over me with his chest bare, he pressed his wadded-up T-shirt to my ear. It was his Poser T-shirt that he wore to school at least twice a week, and he was willingly staunching my blood with it. He must be in love.

More likely, I was having a wet dream. They'd told us during sex-ed week in PE that this might happen to girls as well as to boys. It had never happened to me. And now, just when I'd given up hope because I was seventeen and the puberty thing was pretty much done, here was Nick Krieger tenderly touching my face with the sun setting behind him and snowflakes sliding off his bare shoulders.

"Hayden," he said again, gently. "Are you sure you didn't hit your head?"

"I don't think so." It came out as a whisper. I cleared my throat. "I think it's just my ear." Now that his T-shirt was warming my skin, I could tell the insistent sting came from my earlobe rather than from the cold.

He moved the T-shirt aside and leaned closer, examining my ear. Oooh, it would be so much more romantic if he looked into my eyes rather than fixating on my ear. Shouldn't I be able to make this happen? What was the world coming to, that I couldn't even control what Nick did in my own wet dream?

He poked my ear.

"Ow, ow, ow!" I squealed, and then felt faint again, out of breath. This was no wet dream. It was reality after all.

He let out a disgusted sigh. "Hayden, Josh is right. The doctor might not even put a stitch in that. What's the matter with you? Do you faint at the sight of blood?"

Oh, no. There was no way I would let him get the upper hand, even if I *was* lying on my back in the snow and he was kneeling over me. I laughed. "Of *course* I don't faint at the sight of blood. I jump onto the dance floor and do the Soulja Boy. Get the hell off me, Dr. McDreamy."

He sat back in surprise. I rolled over to all fours and stood up slowly, letting his T-shirt slide off my ear, since my injury was so minor. The woods seemed to tilt sharply to the left.

"Hayden," said Nick. "Take it easy."

"What for? This would never have happened to a boy, right? A boy could break his leg and keep on boarding. So could I." Or maybe not, but at least I could hike out of the trees on my own power after I scratched my ear. It wasn't until I looked down to check my footing that I realized I was still bleeding. *Plop, plop, plop,* neat red circles that burrowed warm holes into the snow.

"Well?" Chloe called from far off. "Is she okay?"

"No, but is she ever?" Nick lifted me.

One of his arms cradled my head against the wad of his T-shirt. He hooked his other strong arm under my knees. His chest felt intensely warm against me. I opened my eyes and saw his chest was still bare. He'd put his flannel shirt and parka back on without fastening them.

He seemed good for a few steps. Then he hit a soft patch of snow. His foot sank, and he staggered. Josh trudged forward to help, struggling with three snowboards—his, Nick's, and mine, I supposed. If Nick fell while carrying me, even if it was due to loose powder, he would blame it on my unwieldiness or my girth. Together with Josh's joke, I would never, ever live it down.

"Let go," I said. "I can walk." At least, that's what I meant to say, but it came out slurred.

"Shut up." Nick took a few more steps. Now we were on Main Street, where the snow pack was solid. His strides were more sure.

"We can't leave the snow all bloody," I told the underside of his chin, shadowed with stubble. "It will scare the tourists."

"The new snow will cover it up." He looked down at me. "Shhh."

Something in his *shhh* tugged at my heart. He kept watching me, not examining my ear for medical emergencies but looking into my eyes, for a few more steps. I couldn't read his look. He was kind of blurry, for one thing, and I was kind of dizzy. I thought he looked . . . concerned. Sympathetic. Determined to rescue me from danger. I wished that was what he felt. But it couldn't have been. I was misreading him.

What did he really think of me? He probably assumed I was faking loss of consciousness. Maybe he even thought I'd cut my ear on purpose, all to get out of the comp without admitting defeat. If he hated me, so be it, but I'd be damned if he hated me by mistake.

"I broke my leg," I breathed.

He stopped short in the snow and glanced down at me again, alarmed this time. His eyes traveled across my body. "I don't think so, Hayden. Where does it hurt?"

I shook my head, which made him squeeze me more tightly to his chest.

"I mean, when I broke my leg before. I broke it in four places. It bled a *lot*. I didn't walk for a year." I said all this in one gasp, rushing through so I didn't pass out again just from thinking about the way my leg had looked when I'd hit the rocks. I hadn't felt anything at first. I was scared I was paralyzed. When the pain hit me a few seconds later, I was actually relieved. And then, not. I'd never felt pain like that, or seen that much blood.

"Hey, don't cry." He sounded horrified. I couldn't see him anymore through the tears, and I was glad.

"Is she crying?" Gavin called from behind us. "Let me see."

"Just go," I sobbed to Nick. "Get me out of here."

"Gavin, be a little more sensitive," Nick grumbled. "Jesus."

"*You're* telling *me* to be *sensitive*?" Gavin called, and then Chloe was scolding him. The snow was heavier now. The clumps of snowflakes were so big that they squeaked as they hit the ground, like rubber-soled shoes on a gym floor. I hated snow like this, even though it would mean wicked boarding in a few days. Snow like this reminded me of a Laura Ingalls Wilder book I'd read when I was little, about plucky Laura stranded in the Western wilderness when the locusts descended, a cloud of millions of locusts stripping the crops clean in a manner of hours. Nothing had filled the air like this in Tennessee.

"You're shaking," Nick said gently. "Are you cold?" He hugged me closer to his warm skin.

"Is she going into shock?" Davis suggested.

"No," I said, "I just . . . I know we're headed to the gondola." In answer, the groans of metal cable against metal gear reached me from across the slope. "I don't ride the gondola." I tried to stop shuddering.

"It's the best way to get you down the hill. You'll have to walk, too, or they'll call the ski patrol." Nick eased me down from his arms, and I stood against him as he buttoned his shirt and zipped his coat. "Okay. Lean on me. Hide that bloody T-shirt and move your hair over your ear."

As we hiked across the snow to the gondola station ahead, I stuffed the Poser shirt into my pocket, then reached up and tentatively touched my ear. "Oh my God, what happened to my luck?"

"Your clover earring?" Nick asked. His low voice sounded even deeper with my head on his chest. I caught a little chill at the nearness of him, shiver upon shiver.

"It got pulled out of your earlobe, Hayden," Chloe offered. "That's why you're bleeding." As we continued to walk, I felt Nick move. I didn't have to look. I knew he moved his hand across his neck, telling Chloe to shut up.

Good idea. A new wave of dizziness hit me. I wasn't sure anymore whether it was the thought of blood or the fear of heights. Either way, I was going to pass out again, here in front of the gondola station for the park officials to see. "I lost my luck," I murmured, waiting with Nick for the next gondola, watching the huge cable slide through the huge gears, listening to the shriek of the machine. "My dad gave me that luck."

"You can make your own luck," Josh called from behind us in line.

"Right!" I exclaimed with new purpose. I needed to get my mind off my phobias and act like a halfway sane person on the gondola. The gondola car slung around the curve of the station and paused just long enough for all of us to pile on. I had my eyes closed and let Nick guide me, but I did step on and slide beside him onto the plastic bench. Like we were a couple.

sick

(sik) *adj*. **1.** good **2.** cool **3.** gnarly **4.** Hayden

The nurse knocked softly on the door of the examining room and wheeled in a shiny silver tray displaying neatly arranged instruments of torture. She handed me a paper cup of water and then a smaller paper cup, shaking it to rattle the pill inside. "Mmmmmm, guess what I okayed with your mother over the phone? It's to calm you down. Take that, then stare at this tray, and call to me when stitches seem like a good idea." She bustled out. I was left with no one for company but the smiling photos of other patients on the bulletin board across the room. Clearly *they* did not need stitches.

Sometimes I was glad my doctor and his staff had a sense of humor. This was one of the times when I was not. Still, I took the pill. Anything was better than yo-yo fainting and waking up to a new humiliation. And after five minutes, or perhaps five hours, I realized I was counting the smiling faces of patients on the bulletin board for the three hundredth time. "Nurse!"

Nick grinned at me from across the wide cab of his SUV, then glanced back at the snowy road, then smiled over at me again. He looked so handsome and mature as the glow of streetlights passed over him and faded.

He said, "You're loaded."

I remembered being carried into Liz's den. If I hadn't talked to my mom on the phone pre-pill and agreed to spend the night with Liz so her mom could watch me, I might not have known where I was. It occurred to me that I should be embarrassed, sleeping in a room full of awake boys. But I wasn't embarrassed, and that was *delicious*. To hell with teen angst. I went back to sleep.

Then I heard gunshots. An action movie was playing on Liz's TV. I recognized Will Smith's voice. Funny, I must have associated the sound of Will Smith with the smell and sensation of Nick. I could have sworn Nick was with me, just as in seventh grade when we'd snuggled together during that fateful romantic-comedy movie. I inhaled him, sighed happily, and sank back into wistful dreams of him.

I woke, but I didn't want to be awake. I kept my eyes closed and listened for what had changed to wake me. The gunshots and explosions in the movie had grown surprisingly soothing after a while. Now they'd given way to the sweeping theme song as the credits rolled, and soft voices around me.

"Is she still asleep?" Liz asked from somewhere across the room.

Closer by, Gavin answered, "If she wasn't, there's no way she could have been quiet this long." A *smack* sounded as Chloe slapped him for insulting me.

Nick's voice was closer still, down at my feet. He was sharing the sofa with me. There must have been nowhere else for him to sit in the room. "I knew she broke her leg before she moved here, but I never realized it was that big a deal."

Oh, no, I really *had* spilled all that to him while woozy! Stupendous. Luckily, I was lying on my side with my face to the back of the sofa, so I wouldn't give myself away with fluttering eyelashes or a grimace. Chloe and Liz confirmed and cooed, and I felt myself drifting off again.

Then something moved on my ankle. I nearly jumped out of my skin. And still another wave of adrenaline rushed through me as I realized what was happening. Nick wasn't just sharing the sofa with me because there was nowhere else to sit in Liz's den. My feet were in his lap. His hand was around my ankle. He was *rubbing my ankle*, his fingertips tracing slow circles around my ankle bone.

Technically, he wasn't even touching me, unless you counted the pressure of his fingers through my sock. It was ridiculous for me to go tense under his hand, hardly daring to breathe, waiting for the next stroke of his fingers. Except that this meant something. I doubted anyone could see Nick touching me from across the darkened room. Nick wasn't doing this for his friends, showing them how he could tease me to get the upper hand with me. He wasn't even doing this for me. He thought I was asleep. He was doing it for himself. He was stroking me, comforting me, putting a protective hand on me, because he wanted to. Even after he'd said he was finished with me.

The conversation moved on to Will Smith and the movie. The TV switched from teen drama to basketball and back as Chloe and Gavin snatched the remote away from each other. I tried to relax a bit and enjoy Nick's hand on my ankle while I had it, because I might not ever experience this strangely intense connection with him again. But I resigned myself to the torture of remaining wide awake and perfectly still for a few more hours until everyone went home.

I started awake, jerking upright this time. The shadowy room was empty. They must have turned off the satellite box but not the TV, and after a few minutes of silence it had burst into static and had woken me. I relaxed against the pillows on the sofa, but the static wouldn't let me ease back to sleep.

It was like my brain, loud and scrambled and panicky.

I peeled myself from the sofa, switched off the TV, and padded through the silent house to the hall bathroom. I squeezed my eyes shut and flicked on the light. Then I opened my eyes slowly to protect them from the glare, but also because I dreaded seeing what I had looked like to Nick while he lugged me around all evening. I couldn't avoid the mirror right in front of me.

My face was pale, my eyes smudged with dark circles underneath, as if I'd spent the last few hours fainting and then sleeping fitfully. Go figure. My normally straight hair had been so teased by hats and goggles and pillows and Nick that it had grown big and frizzy. And my ear—I pushed back my hair to examine the tiny bandage on my earlobe. *This* had caused all the trouble? I felt like a fool.

Frowning at myself, I reached up and fingered my other earlobe and the one lucky earring I had left. I wasn't a fool. Hysterical, yes. Maladjusted, definitely. But not a fool. My broken leg had been a devastating injury. So had my encounter with Nick four years ago. I'd known this, but only now was I realizing just how badly I'd been hurt.

Sighing, I washed my face. I was squeezing toothpaste onto the toothbrush Liz's mom kept there for me, because I always forgot mine, when I heard voices outside. I stepped over to the window and pushed aside the curtain, then backed up a pace when the cold night air leaking around the windowsill touched my skin.

Nick and Gavin were talking at the end of the driveway—or what I assumed, from the tire tracks, was the driveway under a blanket of fresh snow. Streetlights glinted on Nick's dark and Gavin's black hair. Then Gavin got into his car, and Nick hiked through the snow toward his SUV.

"Oh, mo," I mumbled through toothpaste. I couldn't let him get away. Not now.

I swished, spat, and ran for the front door, pausing only to shove my feet into galoshes owned by some unknown member of Liz's family. Her stepdad, I decided as I tried to run down the snowy front steps. The galoshes were so big, it was like wading in a Tennessee river.

I was too late anyway. They were gone.

Gavin's tires spun briefly and his car pulled away, taillights reflecting red and long on the snow. But no—Nick's SUV still sat idling in the street at the end of the driveway. And as I waded closer, I saw he was in the driver's seat of the dark cab, slowly, repeatedly banging his head on the steering wheel.

He must not have heard me approach over the hum of the engine. I walked all the way up to the passenger-side window and stood there, watching him, waiting for him to notice me. He would see that I had caught him banging his head on his steering wheel, and this was something I could tease him about and hold over his head for the next few months at school.

But I was getting cold in my foreign galoshes and only two layers of clothes in the freezing night. As Nick kept hitting his head, I realized the two of us weren't in that place anymore, the one where we made fun of each other and had a fight and left it at that. We'd been driving in circles, having wrecks and backing over each other, but somehow we'd come way past that place in the last week. I knocked on the window.

He stopped with his head halfway to

the steering wheel for another whack, and he turned to me with his eyes wide behind his dark hair. Immediately, he slid across the seat and pulled the handle to open the door for me.

Leaving the galoshes outside in the snow, I gratefully slid inside the warm cab and shut the door softly so it wouldn't wake the neighborhood. Nick took off his parka and draped it around my shoulders. He didn't have to say, "You shouldn't be out here without a coat," or "You shouldn't be awake now after the terrible day you had." I could see all this in his eyes. He wasn't concerned with making a joke at my expense. He was concerned about *me*.

"What were you and Gavin talking about?"

Nick rolled his eyes and let out a frustrated sigh. "He thinks I've wanted to be with you all these years, and his proof is the way I acted when you got hurt today. He says good friends shouldn't lie to each other. He's really lording it over me, too. Such an ass."

"Is he right?" I whispered.

Nick's dark eyes drilled into me, and the set of his jaw hardened. He slipped one hand onto my waist, underneath the parka.

"Uh," I protested.

He put his other hand on the opposite side of my waist.

"Nick," I said.

He slid me toward him across the seat.

"You," I whispered, looking into his eyes.

He was about to kiss me. His lips brushed mine. He pressed down on me with his chest, bent me backward until I lay down across the seat, and he lay on top of me. He closed his eyes, and the tip of his nose touched mine in an Eskimo kiss. Then he opened his eyes, stared hard at me, and went still. "You want to make out and then have an argument?" he whispered.

"Yes," I said. It would be worth it.

"You sure?"

I swallowed. "Absolutely."

"Then tell me what happened when you broke your leg, and why you're so terrified of heights after all this time."

I looked up into his dark eyes. I wanted to say something, but his weight was heavy on my chest, and I could hardly breathe.

"I broke my leg." Suddenly the story gushed out of me. "I was eleven. I loved outdoorsy sports. My parents let me go to adventure camp up in the mountains in

Tennessee. My first day there, I fell."

That moment had flashed through my mind so many times since, it was as much a part of me as my lungs or my heart or my red hair, and I couldn't describe it to Nick. The long fall, with repeated jerks upward as safety mechanisms caught me and then failed. Realizing I was on the ground. Wondering why I wasn't hurt. Trying to stand. Seeing all the blood, and then my leg. The slowly growing horror that continued to build over the next few days until I reached my breaking point.

Between our bodies and the seat of the SUV, Nick squeezed my hand.

I gasped. "In Tennessee I was known as the girl who came in a wheelchair to the Valentine's dance. The girl whose friends had to go out of their way to include her when they went to a concert or the mall. At first, I counted myself lucky to have friends like that. But a couple of times I overheard them arguing about why they always had to invite me when it was such a pain to find the wheelchair ramps everywhere we went. They said it would be so much easier to flirt with boys if they weren't always worried about *me*.

"And then, one day when I'd made it out of the wheelchair and onto crutches, I gimped into the room and caught them imitating me. I didn't see enough of it that I recognized myself, but I could tell from everyone else's stricken expressions that they thought I had. It was so foreign. I used to be in charge of things, like Chloe. I was president of the fifth grade class. And I used to make good grades like Chloe and Liz. Gosh, it's hard to think back that far. Fifth grade math must have been a lot easier than eleventh grade math."

"You think?" Nick's words were dry, but his tone was gentle.

"I had never been that girl people made fun of. I didn't want to be that girl. I am not that girl."

He watched me, wishing he had never asked this question, wondering what possessed him to break up with somebody easy like Fiona.

But no—with tentative fingers, he brushed a strand of my hair away from my forehead.

And for just a moment, I really wasn't that girl. I had never been that girl. I was that cool teenager again, who moved to a new town and found a new boyfriend. The girl who started over.

I sniffled. "By the time we moved here, I was walking without a limp. People had no idea. I was only the new girl, the red-haired girl, the girl who Nick Krieger made a fool of."

If Nick hadn't been holding my hand, I would have slapped it over my mouth. This *was* what I thought, but it's not what I'd intended to share with Nick right then.

His eyes widened in shock. Sorrow moved across his face, and then worry. "I wanted to tell you, Hayden. Yes, I had a bet with Gavin in seventh grade, and you wandered into it. But I really liked you. I wished Liz had never told you about the bet, and we could have stayed together."

"Why didn't you come clean with me when you figured out you liked me?"

He sighed, a short, disdainful puff through his nose. "I was thirteen."

I wasn't buying it. "You had a bet. You couldn't lose a bet. If you have a choice between me and winning, you'll choose winning every time. It's still true."

The worried expression on his face morphed into anger. He let go of my hand

and sat up, his chest heavier on mine just before his weight lifted from me completely. "You are *not* going to put this on me," he barked.

"I'm not trying to put anything on you." I backed across the seat and scooted up to sit against the door.

"You can blame me or your fall or whatever you want for not being able to go off that jump. But the bottom line is, some people are competitors and some people aren't. There's no way you're suddenly going to decide at age seventeen to become a competitor. You don't have it in you. You're just scared."

I would have been mad at Nick for saying this to me at any time. But right now, after I'd spent the night fainting and I desperately needed comfort, I was downright bitter. "Me!" I lashed out. "You're one to talk. You're scared to tell your father that you made a mistake, agreeing to this challenge with me. *You're* the coward." I opened the door to a swirl of frigid air, remembered I was still wearing Nick's parka, and struggled out of it.

"That's bullshit." He grabbed the back of the parka, but I got the distinct impression he was not trying to be a gentleman by helping me out of it. He just wanted his parka back. "When you feel cornered, you'll just fling whatever you've got at people, and you don't care who gets hurt with what."

"I am not scared." I slid down from the truck seat into Liz's stepdad's galoshes, then turned to face Nick one last time. "I am not scared of boarding *or* you, and I will prove it to you tomorrow. If you think I'm going easy on you in the comp just because you have a debilitating injury from yesterday—"

"That's what you think," he snarked. "I've been doing yoga."

"—you have another think coming. You will buy me those Poser tickets. And I'm not even taking you. You will hand the tickets over to me, and I'll take someone else."

"Who? Your little brother's friends?"

"No, Everett Walsh." I closed the door softly behind me so as not to alarm sleeping adults, because I was that mature.

Even through the door and the rolled up window, I could clearly hear every filthy word Nick uttered, ending with, "Everett [cuss word] Walsh."

I opened the passenger door. "Ask not for whom the fire-crotch burns; it burns for thee!" I'd meant this to be an insult. Then I realized it sounded like I wanted Nick. Or like I had a feminine problem.

"Shut up," Nick said. "I'm waiting for you to go in the house."

"Fine." I slammed his door, forgetting all about courtesy to sleeping adults this time. But as I hiked back through the yard to Liz's front porch, I was so proud of myself for not crying. I never shed a tear.

Not until I opened the front door and heard his truck ease away. Just as he'd promised, he'd idled there all that time, watching me, waiting to make sure I got inside the house okay. Like a gentleman.

I closed the door softly, turned the deadbolt, and managed to slip out of the galoshes and line them up against the wall as I'd found them. Only then, with everything else in order, did the tears spill out of me. I wanted to scream, but there was no way I'd startle everyone in the house like that. Holding the sobs inside hurt my ribs. I collapsed on the floor, hugging my knees, rocking back and forth on the carpet. I felt empty, lost, and totally alone in the dark house.

I wished I could start over in a new town, with new friends. I would do everything right this time.

No, wait. That's exactly the chance I'd had four years ago, and now I'd blown it.

Besides, just thinking about leaving Liz and Chloe and Nick behind, I missed them already.

I was exhausted, even after so many hours of fainting and drug-induced sleep. My first instinct was to lie back on the carpet where I sat. But that might alarm Liz's mom when she woke up to make breakfast. She would trip over me like I was Doofus. The obvious choice was the den sofa, which I could see from my seat on the floor. But Nick's scent would linger there. Thoughts of him touching me might have lulled me to sleep earlier this evening. They would keep me wide awake now.

In the end I dragged myself down the hall and up the stairs to Liz's room. Chloe snored softly in one twin bed. Liz was sprawled across the other. Lifting Liz's covers, I tried to coax her over so I could slide in next to her. With gentle prodding, she wouldn't budge. It was exactly like the last time I'd had a nightmare about falling and had wandered down to get in bed with my mother. Liz finally groaned and gave me some room. I lay down beside her, relaxed into her warmth, and felt comforted just lying next to her, even if she didn't know I was there.

She rolled over and spooned against me, fitting her front to my back. She draped her arm across me and hugged. "You okay?" she whispered dreamily.

I nodded. "I thought Nick and I were going to make out."

"Surprise."

"And then we had a fight. If you and Chloe could throw us together, I would really appreciate it, because I don't know how to fix this anymore."

"Tell us about it in the morning."

I nodded again, then felt myself sobbing, shaking against Liz. She held me more tightly as I cried myself to sleep.

steeze

(stēz) *n.* **1.** style and ease **2.** you've either got it or you don't

After a big breakfast at Liz's house and more bitching with her and Chloe about what pigs boys could be, I rode the bus home to change into clean boarding clothes. I walked into the mud room—tripped over Doofus—and found Josh stepping into his boarding boots. "Hey!" I greeted him cheerfully. "Thanks for coming to my rescue yesterday, and for calling me fat."

"You're going to be sorry you were snide to me when you see what I've got for you."

He lifted the folded garment next to him and shook it out.

The BOY TOY jeans!

"What do you mean?" I exclaimed. "They're mine *forever*?"

"Yes. They're to help you make your own luck. The catch is, if you want them forever, you have to wear them to the comp today."

"But I'll get soaked!" I wailed.

"Don't fall."

I took the jeans from him and hugged them close. "Thank you, Josh. This means so much to me. I know you've joked about me going pro and taking you with me, but are you actually *for* me in this comp? I figured you'd have a bet with Gavin's sister that I'd lose."

He shook his head. "I went ahead and bought her and me both a ticket. Might as well. That's one bet I know I'd lose."

"Aww, Josh, that's so awesome of you!" I wrapped my arms around him and hugged him hard.

He didn't hug me back. He stiffened and said, "Ew, ew, ew."

I let him go and stepped back to look him in the eye.

"Ew," he said again. But one corner of his mouth crooked upward in a smile.

It was nice to have at least one boy behind me.

"Hayden O'Malley!"

I looked up from the sink and peered around the women's bathroom in the ski lodge. Chicks stood inside and outside stalls, in various states of undress. Waterproof layers were hard to get in and out of, and snowboarders definitely were not peeless goddesses. Finally I saw the girl who had called my name. She stood in the doorway, long blond hair twisted into hippie twirls and braids.

"Daisy Delaney!" I hollered.

"I'd recognize you anywhere!" she yelled over the chatter in the bathroom. "They're playing your steeziness over and over on local TV! Girl, you're famous!" She crossed the room and leaned forward to hug me by way of introduction.

We talked for a few minutes about the local competition I'd won and the tricks I'd landed. Then she said, "After your comp is over, my boyfriend and I are shredding the back bowls. Want to hang? We can get a head start on your lessons next week, see where you are. I can give you some pointers." She chuckled. "Maybe *you* can give *me* some pointers."

"The back bowls? Sure!" I felt confident that she wouldn't find out what a chicken I was, because after the comp, if I hadn't gone off the jump, I would be dead of shame. And if I *had* gone off the jump, I would be just plain dead.

"Your friend Chloe told me this comp is with your ex," she said. "What's *that* about? Are you hooking up again or what?"

"Not anymore," I said wistfully. "Can I ask you something? This whole argument started because he said I couldn't beat an average boy snowboarder. Does it bother you that your boyfriend has landed a 1260 in competition and you haven't?"

"So this is a girl-power thing?" Daisy mused.

"It's a lot more complicated than that, but that's how it started."

She shrugged as best she could in her puffy outerwear. "I might land a 1080. I might not. But I'm sure not going to give up boarding just because the odds are stacked against me to be the best boarder ever. I mean, there are short people who play professional basketball."

"True."

"And on a personal level, my boyfriend and I love each other enough, and we have enough respect for each other, that we're bigger than that."

I laughed. "Nick and I are not bigger than that. We are very, very small."

Daisy nodded. "And then, of course, there's the fact that I'm prettier than my boyfriend. He may fly higher, but I look better doing it." She turned around backward. "I mean, even in these snow pants, check out my ass."

We both cackled, and everyone in the bathroom stared at us. I decided right then that Daisy was going to be fun to hang out with, and I could learn a lot from her.

When I'd envisioned the comp with Nick, I'd pictured exactly this strong sunshine and bright blue sky. Beyond that, my predictions were all wrong. I'd thought my friends and Nick's friends would be waiting for us at the bottom of Main Street. I hadn't imagined a crowd of several hundred people, as many as had watched the local competition last Tuesday. They rang bells for Nick and me because they couldn't clap in their mittens, cheering for us as we boarded over to the ski lift.

I also hadn't realized I'd have to ride up on the lift with Nick, just the two of us. But it was the last Saturday of winter break. The slopes were crowded. Nobody got to ride a lift alone. And he was right behind me in line. Nick and me riding up together right then was like George W. Bush and Barack Obama riding to Obama's inauguration in the same limo. Relaxed!

We didn't say a word to each other the whole time we shuffled through the long line in the shed. Finally it was our turn. We slid into position in the path of the chair. It swept us off our feet and up into the air, and Nick pulled the guard bar down across our laps.

After the voices echoing in the shed, the cold air around us was silent, except for the ski-lift cable clanking overhead and the *swish* of skiers dodging moguls below us.

I looked up at Nick beside me. He had his goggles down already. I couldn't see his eyes behind those damn reflective lenses.

I took in a sharp breath of freezing air.

"I'm not saying this because I'm scared, or because I want to get out of anything. But I want you to know that I'm sorry for what happened between us last night. We've said a lot of ugly things to each other in the past week, and we didn't mean most of them." I raised my voice as we neared a pole supporting the lift, and the cable clanked louder and louder through the pulleys. "At least, *I* didn't. If we can just get past all this, I think we're both bigger than that."

Now I found I was shouting, even though the noise of the cable had died away. Even more deafening was Nick's silence. He didn't look down at me, didn't say a word as we passed four more poles and boarded off the lift. I could see a muscle working under his skin in his strong superhero jaw, but his mouth stayed closed.

We slid to the top of a narrow slope that curved into the forest. "Hey," Nick called to a kid boarding by. "We're racing. Say go, would you?"

The kid turned to us, and his eyes widened. "Oh my God, you're Nick Krieger and Hayden O'Malley, aren't you? Is this the comp everybody's been talking about? Are you guys hooking up?"

"Just say go!" Nick and I both yelled.

"Go!" the kid shouted.

I pointed myself downhill and boarded as fast as I could. But it was no use. A field of rumble strips slowed me down like speed bumps for a car. Nick was so much bigger than me that he blazed straight across them like they weren't there. Soon the slope took a turn into the forest and he disappeared behind the trees. He was gone, baby.

I was boarding by myself. I kept going as fast as I could, crouching down into the frigid wind and squinting through the water on my goggles, just so the spectators at the bottom didn't tire of waiting for me, give up, and go home, thinking I'd forfeited. No way.

The trees fell away on either side of me, and the slope opened up wide. At the bottom of the course where it merged with Main Street, I picked out Nick, one of the tallest boys, already standing in the crowd with his arms crossed, watching for me as if he'd been waiting all day. Then the three judges with their heads together. Then a gaggle of girls with Liz and Chloe in front, gloves over their mouths, watching for me.

So I did what the most stylish boardercross riders do when they're not winning but they know they've got the silver in the bag. I hit the last roller and cranked it into a front flip, a little steeze for the fangirls. The second I landed, the girls hit me with an ear-splitting squeal laced with frantic bell-ringing. I couldn't help breaking into the widest smile. I skidded to a stop in front of them.

Daisy leaned over to bump fists with me. "Girl has attitude. *Way* to *lose*!"

I laughed nervously and said, "Thanks." I wasn't sure if this was a compliment.

Liz guided Chloe over so Chloe didn't lose her balance and hurt anyone. They both gave me big hugs, and Chloe shook me by the shoulders. "We're down but we're not out. Go back up there and give him hell."

"Thanks, coach!" I slid away from the crowd and over to the lift again, following Nick. I didn't want to linger with Chloe and Liz, because I knew the crowd was wait-ing expectantly. But if I'd had more time, I would have asked for coaching on the sitch with Nick.

We moved through the line in the shad-owy shed and launched into the sunshine in the chair again. I prepared for another cold, silent ride. His goggles were up this time, but I didn't look over at him and try to read the expression in his eyes. I was afraid it would break my heart.

"I'm sorry, too," he said.

At first I thought it was wishful thinking on my part, and I'd misheard him. But then he slid his glove onto my thigh. Even through the BOY TOY jeans, I felt those familiar tingles shooting up my leg.

"You *are?*" I exclaimed. "Why didn't you say something before? I was all worried!"

"I didn't want you to think I was apologizing because of the comp. You know, we want this to be fair and square so we don't have to go through it again."

"Then why are you copping to it now?"

"Because I don't want you to think I hate you. I don't hate you. I definitely don't." He squeezed my thigh.

"But you still think I'm not a competitor," I muttered. I was trying to be bigger than this, but there was no getting around it. If Nick and I were going to ease toward being together again, I wanted him to respect me.

"No, I do." He turned to me for the first time, and his dark eyes searched my eyes. "Did you know the local TV channel broadcasts your 900 in an endless loop? It's a bunch of video want ads for snowmobiles, then some kind of school crap with Everett Walsh that nobody wants to see over and over, and then you. I stayed up watching you until three o'clock this morning." He gave me that brilliant smile. "You're a competitor all right. I just wasn't sure you realized it yourself. And I never would have said something like that to you if I didn't consider you a true friend."

I put my mitten over his glove and squeezed. I wasn't sure whether he was hinting at a relationship or not. I hoped, if we were this big as people, we could be even bigger, and could take another shot at getting together. But I was thankful just to count him as a friend.

We slid off the lift and boarded down to the top of the half-pipe. The bell-ringing crowd had moved to the sides and bottom of the course. It seemed to have grown.

Nick pulled his goggles down over his eyes and nosed his board to the edge of the slope.

"Good luck," I called. "And be careful."

"Are you kidding? I do yoga to stay limber,

so I won't get hurt. I did thirty minutes of Sun Salutations this morning."

He balanced on the deck, then sped down into the bowl and up the opposite side, momentum flinging him high into the blue sky. Six times, he executed simple but perfect tricks with incredible height. He might just beat me. If I fell in my BOY TOY jeans, I was toast. Very soggy toast.

But whether I won or not, I looked forward to my run. A half-pipe course was the best part of my day, an unbelievably decadent treat, like white cake with white icing that said CONGRATULATIONS HAYDEN! Sliding forward for my turn was like taking that first bite of sugar rush.

Following Nick's path, I raced down one wall and up the other. The slopes were crowded enough today, and enough kids had already gone through the pipe that morning, that the fresh powder had been worked into perfection for a smooth, fast run. I threw a few respectable tricks, then pulled out my specialties: back-to-back sevens, a McTwist, and my beloved nine. I hated for it to end. I would have loved to lay down just one more 720, but I ran out of pipe.

I slid straight across the flat toward the

crowd and pulled up in front of them, strategically sending a wave of powder over the boys. The girls were already cheering for me and ringing their bells wildly (so cute!), but when I sent that powder flying, their cheers hurt my ears.

"You're neck and neck," Daisy called from where she stood with the other judges. "Hayden destroyed this one."

The huge pack of boys moaned. "What about Nick's massive air?" Gavin called.

"Hayden landed a 900," Chloe retorted. "That's bananas!"

I was happy I'd tied Nick, at least so far. I certainly wasn't going to hang around and gloat about it—not when I was about to get shown up in the big air comp. I was following Nick around the edge of the crowd to take the ski lift again when Daisy boarded over to me.

She put her head down and talked quietly, so only I could hear her above the excited crowd. "You've got this nice, quiet, compact style that competition judges are going to *love*, and then you add a nine? That's sick. The only thing we're going to work on in your lessons is height, because judges want to see that too. If you can land a nine going as low as you do, imagine what you'll put down when you're going huge like Kelly Clark. You're on your way, girlfriend. And you're mine!"

"Hooray!" I exclaimed. Never mind that I'd developed my compact style precisely because I didn't want to go too huge and lose my balance. Daisy and I locked forearms and jumped up and down together excitedly, or as well as we could manage with boards on. Then I high-fived Chloe and Liz as I passed them in the crowd, and I followed Nick.

When I boarded even with him, I asked, "Did you get all that with me and Daisy?"

He laughed. "I got enough."

"No pressure." We both cracked up.

But through our laughter, I thought I heard someone calling Nick. I touched his arm and nodded to the deck of the ski lodge. "It's your dad."

"Oh God," Nick said under his breath. "Not just my dad but his corporate partners. Beer before lunch is never a good thing. Come with me and save my ass."

I definitely did not want to talk with Nick's dad and two other men in the most expensive skiwear, drinking beer around a snow-covered table. But Nick needed me. We stopped at the wooden railing.

"Nick!" they called in big, strong, Manly Corporate Partner voices.

Nick nodded, wearing his own Big Man On Campus grin. "Dad, you remember Hayden. Mr. Jeter, Mr. Black, this is my girlfriend, Hayden."

I smiled sweetly at them and shook hands with them when they stood and extended their arms over the rail. This took my mind off the fact that my face was as red as my hair (Nick seemed to have that effect on me a *lot*) and the fact that NICK KRIEGER HAD JUST CALLED ME HIS GIRLFRIEND!

"You let a girl beat you?" one of them asked Nick with a twinkle in his eye. I think he meant this to be charming. "Must be true love."

If my face had turned red before, now it was probably turning purple. I was glad I couldn't see it. At least my freckles were obscured for once.

"Oh, no sir," Nick said. "I didn't let her beat me. Hayden's so much better than I am, she's in a different league. She's going pro soon."

"Then why'd you challenge her?" Mr.

Krieger asked. His words went along with the jovial banter of the moment. But behind the words, I heard his tone, the same bitter tone he'd used to talk about Nick when Doofus and I had crashed into his living room. He wanted Nick to win, no matter what, and Nick would hear about this again when he got home.

"Oh, he didn't challenge me," I piped up. "I challenged him, and Nick is always so supportive. He wants me to be the best I can be." This was all the corporate lingo I knew.

"But Mr. Jeter," Nick said, "about it being true love, you're absolutely right." He turned to me.

He kissed me on the forehead.

In front of his father and two corporate partners.

"Nice to see you, gentlemen," Nick said formally. Then he slid away. Rather than standing there dazed, I scrambled to follow him.

As soon as we were out of their earshot, he bent toward me. "Hayden! Good schmoozing!" he crowed.

I think he was referring to my handling of his dad's partners. However, I was still thinking about his soft lips on my forehead. I said, "I'll say."

"I hope I set a good example for my dad," Nick said. "He's flying down to Phoenix tonight for a Valentine's date with my mother."

"Nick, that's so great!" I squealed. Wait a minute. It was great that Nick's parents were making an effort to get back together. But did Nick mean that's the only reason he'd kissed me? That was not great at all!

The crowd had paused when we stopped to talk to Nick's dad, but now they moved with us toward the jump. I noticed a couple of film crews had arrived, probably from the resort and the local TV station. No pressure.

An out-of-control Chloe barreled out of the crowd, dragging Liz by the hand. They threatened to run me down. Nick caught Chloe by the hand as she slid past, and Liz was able to swing them both around in front of me.

"We'll go up the lift with you for moral support, Hayden," Chloe said. "We'll coach you off the jump."

"Great. Thank you!" I said, shaking imaginary snow out of my hair. I couldn't give Liz a meaningful look through my goggles, but I hoped she would get the message. I did not want Chloe's "help." Not today.

"Let's wait for her at the bottom, Chloe," Liz suggested. "That way we won't distract her, and we can hug her when she wins. Come on!" They followed the rest of the crowd sliding toward the bottom of the jump, leaving Nick and me to go up the lift alone.

As soon as the chair left the ground, he said quietly, "I'm going to give you the speech the football coach gives us."

I sniffed a long noseful of cold air. "Okay."

"Everything up until now has been practice," he said. "Regardless of how good or how bad you've looked in practice, you're starting over now. The game is what matters. And a single game has never meant more than this one means to you."

"True." Going off this jump might make the difference between my career as a professional snowboarder and my life in a convent.

So I should have been focusing on the trick I was about to do, *not* on the warmth of Nick beside me, soaking through my BOY TOY jeans and long underwear and into my thigh.

I wondered whether kissing my forehead and calling me his girlfriend and talking about true love were really all just examples for his father, or whether Nick had meant them.

"Speaking of starting over," he said quietly. "Hayden, can you and I start over?"

I looked up at him in astonishment.

He grinned, and I wished I could see his eyes behind his goggles. "I would rather walk across hot coals than go through seventh grade again, I have to tell you. I mean, can we say that everything up until now between you and me has been practice?"

Staring up at his superhero jaw, I enjoyed the tingles spreading across my chest and savored the moment. These were the words I'd waited for him to say since he'd sat next to me in the hall eight days before. I scooted toward him as well as I could with my board hanging heavily from my feet. "Absolutely. I'm ready to play this game with you."

He kissed me, his warm mouth on my mouth. This didn't work very well with his goggles hitting mine, so he pulled up mine and I pulled up his, and we kissed more deeply. It wasn't the most private kiss we'd ever shared, or the longest, or the most romantic. But it mattered the most. Our connection mattered. When we reached the station and boarded off the lift, my heart was racing like I'd just finished the slalom.

We couldn't stop grinning at each other as we returned downhill to the jump. We pulled up, adjusted our goggles, and gazed down the long slope at the white ramp jutting into the clear blue sky. Beyond that, way down the hill, the crowd was even bigger than it had been at the half-pipe. They were very far away, but I thought I recognized my parents' ski clothes, which they didn't pull out of storage very often. They must have gotten back from Boulder and come out to support my comp—what great parents! And ever so faintly, I could hear Josh rapping to his posse's beat. I couldn't make out most of what he was saying, but I thought I caught the word *prepubescent*.

"Do you want to go first?" Nick asked me.

"No, I want you to go first." I wanted to see what trick he landed. Might as well pile as much pressure on myself as possible.

And, truth be told, I wanted to know that I could do this jump all by myself, without him up here coaching me.

"Okay, pep talk before I go." He put his gloves on my shoulders and squeezed. "Don't look at the crowd down there. Don't think about the jump at all. Concentrate on the sick trick you'll do when you go off." He pressed his goggles to my goggles. "Feel the 900."

"900!" I scoffed. "I'm feeling the 1080."

He let me go and stood back, eyeing me. I could tell he didn't want to say anything to destroy my confidence, but he was afraid he'd created a monster.

"Don't worry. I'm ready to play the game." I nodded solemnly.

"One more thing," he said. "If you do fall—"

I cringed. Some pep talk!

"—if something terrible happens, you still won't lose everything. Now you have good friends, and nothing will ever change that. You're *not* that girl."

"Oh, Nick." I threw myself at him, literally. He wrapped me in his arms and brushed my hair aside to kiss my forehead again.

I squeezed him hard, then drew away and punched him on his padded arm. "Go ahead, and *don't* break a leg."

Without fanfare, he steered onto the slope and sped off the jump. A nice 540, or possibly even a 720! I couldn't see his rotations when he disappeared over the edge.

Anyway, all that really mattered to me was that he landed safely. I boarded a few feet to one side and leaned over until I saw him downhill, sliding to a stop, upright. The crowd all waved their arms, and faintly I heard their bells and voices.

My turn. I could do this. I inhaled through my nose and felt my lungs fill with air. My blood spread the life-giving oxygen throughout my body.

I exhaled through my mouth and felt gravity pull the energy from my heart down through my legs, through my boots and snowboard, through the snow, to the rocks below. I was one with the mountain.

I touched my remaining lucky earring.

Then I pressed all my weight forward for speed and raced toward the jump, the white edge, the blue sky beyond, the town below, the mountains in the distance. I went off.

Dancing at the Poser concert had been fun at first, but then Josh and his posse pulled Nick and me into the mosh pit. We needed a break. While Nick snagged us a lawn chair on the ski lodge deck above the concert, I bought us a couple of hot chocolates—and passed Gavin and Chloe at the teller machine. She rubbed her gloves together gleefully, then held them out while Gavin counted the cash into her hands.

"Hayden!" she exclaimed as I walked up, but her eyes didn't leave the money. Clearly, she didn't trust Gavin. "I went ahead and bought us tickets to be safe in case the concert was sold out, and now Gavin is paying—me—back—ha!" She tapped his cheek playfully with the stack of bills. He closed one eye against the attack.

"*Not* that you thought I would lose or anything," I said suspiciously.

She innocently fluttered her eyelashes at me. "Of course not!"

"We shouldn't have doubted you," Gavin said. "I have never seen anybody short of a pro ride the pipe like that."

I glared at him. Because the words were coming from his mouth, I expected them to be sarcastic. But his face was friendly and open. For once, he seemed genuine.

"And a 1080 off the jump?" he went on. "That was savage."

Chloe widened her eyes at him. "Why are you being nice? Has your body been taken over by aliens?"

"You'll find out tonight, baby."

I stopped the tickle fest I felt coming on between them by handing them each a hot chocolate. "Hold this. My phone's beeping." I took it out of my pocket and peered at the text message.

Nick: Do u want 2 b n people?

"*People*," I murmured as if he could hear me. "As in the magazine?" I peered up onto the deck and saw him standing next to our lounge chair, talking with a group of adults with cameras. "Oh my God, paparazzi? No way!"

"Way," Gavin said. "I saw them talking to Daisy Delaney earlier. They must have followed Poser here, then realized there were more celebrities they could milk."

"Nick isn't that kind of celebrity," I said.

"I'll bet they want him for a special theme issue," Chloe suggested. "How the richest bachelors in America spent Valentine's Day."

I glanced dubiously toward the mosh pit. Then I looked toward Nick again and strained to hear what he was saying over the Poser tune.

"Are you here alone?" one of the men asked him. "Are you seeing anyone?"

"Yes, I'm seeing someone," Nick said, standing beside them but hardly acknowledging them. He was watching for my answer on his phone.

"For how long?" a woman asked.

About an hour, I thought. Or did we officially start seeing each other on the ski lift this morning? *Ten hours.* I smiled, remembering the sunny afternoon we'd spent boarding with Daisy Delaney and her boyfriend. Or . . . what did "seeing each other" mean, anyway? If nearly making out in the sauna counted, we'd been seeing each other for five days.

"Four years," I heard him say.

"Aww!" I squealed. Then I turned to Chloe. "Do I want to be in *People?*"

"No," she said firmly. "Nick is hot."

Gavin frowned and poked her in the side. "Hey."

She ducked away from his finger. "Facts are facts. Nick is hot, and when girls read *People* and see he's dating you, they will call you a skank ho. You and I have mooned over Prince William. We know the deal."

"True." When Nick glanced slyly down at me, I shook my head no.

For a few more minutes, I talked with Chloe and Gavin, and we all watched Liz and Davis swaying romantically to a rare slow song from Poser. What a happy Valentine's Day. Then, when the paparazzi had cleared out, I climbed the steps to the deck and handed a cup of hot chocolate to Nick. He sat down in the lawn chair and unzipped his parka. I settled back against his warm shirt.

"I bought you a Valentine's Day present," he said in my ear, sending shivers through me despite all my layers. He rocked to one side in the chair and pulled something from his back pocket.

I took it in my gloved hands and peered at it in the dusky light from the stage and the stars. It was a sew-on patch with a black diamond in the center, the symbol for a dangerous ski slope. "Nick, that's so cool! I love it!"

"That's not all." He rocked to his other side and pulled out another patch. This one had a four-leaf clover. "To replace the luck you're missing."

"Nick." I stared at the patches in my mittens, trying not to tear up. "This is sweet of you."

"I really like you in those 'boy toy' jeans," he said, "but this needs to go on top of 'boy.'" He took the black diamond from me and shook it. "And the clover goes on top of 'toy.'"

"Deal." I slipped the patches into my coat pocket. Then I sipped my hot chocolate and sighed, enjoying his warmth behind me. "We've been dating for four years, huh? I don't think Fiona will like that answer."

"You've always had my heart." He kissed my earlobe—the one without a bandage. The one that was still lucky. "You know, you're going to be in *People* anyway when you make the Olympic snowboarding team. ESPN will ask you, 'Hayden O'Malley, you came from nowhere at age seventeen. Where have you been?' And you'll answer, 'Oh, I had a few acrophobic issues to work through.'"

Laughing, I poked him for his embarrassingly accurate imitation of my Southern drawl.

He continued in my voice, "'Then one night my boyfriend was being an ass and I challenged him to a comp. I had to do a front 1080 off a jump just to show him up, and the rest is history.'"

"I hope so."

"I know so." He kissed my cheek.

I reached back to run my fingers through his long hair. "Right now I want to lie low, have a normal life, and hang out with my boyfriend. I'll meet you in *People* in a few years."

He chuckled, making my insides sparkle with anticipation. "It's a date."

About the Author

Jennifer Echols is the author of the romantic comedies *The Boys Next Door* and *Major Crush* and the teen drama *Going Too Far*. She lives in Alabama with her family, no snow, and a vivid imagination. Please visit her on the Web at www.jennifer-echols.com!

LOL at this sneak peek of

Perfect Shot
By Debbie Rigaud

A new Romantic Comedy from Simon Pulse

★

"Heads up!" was my only warning before it was launched over the aisle toward me. Even though I was on one knee, stocking shelves with acrylic paint tubes, my reflexes were on their feet. My long forearms met the ball of rubber bands with a force that sent it hurling back toward where it came from.

"Ouch!" Pam, my coworker-slash-best-friend, yelped.

Snickering to myself, I rushed over to her aisle to apologize. She gave me the dramatic, injured look, so I knew it wouldn't be easy.

"C'mon, it was just a few *soft* rubber bands," I offered sweetly.

"Yeah—and *not* a volleyball." She pouted, rubbing her forehead. "I swear, London, from now on, going to one of your volleyball matches is gonna feel like watching a scary movie."

"Seeing as how you overact worse than a

Hollyweird D-lister," I teased, "that would be a step up for you."

Pam forgot about her wounded act and coughed up a boisterous laugh that I'm sure all of northern New Jersey heard. She's not usually the loud type, but the girl *is* known to turn up the volume on just about every aspect of her personality.

"You're never gonna let me live that down, huh?" Pam placed her hand—the one not holding a stack of colored pencils—over her heart and squinted as if the sun was in her eyes. "I did it for you. The ref had to understand how foul his call was."

Her theatrics aside, I appreciate that she comes to almost every one of my home games to show her support.

"Mmm-hmm," I teased. "Next time you get the urge to run screaming across the court during game time, don't do me any favors."

"Owww," Pam whimpered. Going for the right distraction to change the subject, she started stroking her forehead again. I grinned and wrapped my long arms around Pam's shoulders, giving her a quick, apologetic squeeze. My five-foot-ten frame extended half a head taller than her.

"Sorry." I picked up the rubber orb and carefully pulled off the red band on top. "Anyway, I only asked you for *one*."

"Next time I won't be so generous." Pam got in the last word before she carried on placing colored pencils into separate slots on a fixture.

I smiled to myself and headed back to my acrylic paint duties. Without intending it to be, working the same shift at Art Attack was becoming the perfect chance for Pam and me to hang together. Even though we're both sophomores at Teawood High, my volleyball season being in full swing and Pam's double passions for fashion *and* her boyfriend, Jake, have kept us preoccupied. Before this job, we'd mostly been keeping in touch via text.

Unexpected bonus BFF time aside, Pam got me a job here for another reason altogether. Once she heard I was passed up for the volleyball summer camp scholarship and had to raise the fifteen-hundred-dollar fee on my own, she put in a good word with her boss. Now here I am, two weeks later, proudly rocking the faux-paint-splattered red employee vest.

Art Attack was one of a few artsy stores

to pop up on Main Avenue in recent months. The eleven-block strip, known to locals as "the Ave," always had potential. Just a few miles from New York City, Teawood, New Jersey, is a large suburb with a metropolitan vibe. Cozy coaches—or as we like to call them, adult school buses—make their way down the Ave, shuttling Teawood residents to and from their NYC jobs every workday, morning and evening. On Saturdays kids either head across the bridge to shop in Manhattan or parade down the Ave in celebs-on-a-coffee-run attire. For them it's all about comfy boots with oversize hand-bags and shades.

In the heart of the strip, the brick side-walks are spacious and lined with benches and old-world lampposts. Luxury car dealer-ships, designer shoe stores, and fancy eve-ning gown showrooms stand alongside busy restaurants, open-late ice cream shops, and trendy clothing stores. Lots of famous folks who live in nearby, more upscale towns—including a few rappers who pub-licly claim to still be living in New York City—can be spotted shopping or lunching here. (Reverend Run's kids are known to pass through, reality-show cameras in tow.)

Shiny cars cruise up and down, looking for both attention and parking.

No celebrity sightings in Art Attack to report yet. That's probably because my part-time working hours are spent avoiding customers and their art-related questions. Pam, in her arstyliciousness, is a much better fit for this job. Honestly, if I'd known that a prerequisite for working at an art supply store was creativity, I would've found another way to earn money.

But it's all worth it. The Peak Performance Volleyball Camp in upstate New York trains top high school players from the tri-state area and gives them a shot at making the national team. I've wanted to go to Peak Performance ever since my gym teacher told me about it in the eighth grade. It has the best reputation. Plus it lands athletes on the radar of prominent college scouts—which is right where I want to be.

Trust, I would walk around stuffed to the gills in grills like rapper Plies if you told me gold teeth had transmitters that blip on the radar of college scouts.

Crazy ambition aside, what's fun about Peak Performance is that after weeks of intensive training in the art of spiking, blocking, serving, and winning, the camp squad flies to Miami to play against teams from other regions across the country.

Even though scholarships were awarded to only two star athletes from my school— seniors who have already been handpicked to play volleyball in college—I was selected to join the camp. My parents said they'd gladly pay the hefty fee . . . but only if I enroll the summer *after* my junior year. Trouble is, who even knows what chance I'd have for getting picked next year! Considering there's no guaranteed placement, I just can't pass up this summer's opportunity.

So for now I'm all about improving my game, which, as it turns out, has been the therapy I needed to get over my ex-boyfriend Rick Stapleton. *Correction:* I didn't need to get over *him* so much as the humiliation of being dumped publicly. Of course, all of that intensified volleyball focus has reflected on my wardrobe (I pair a v-ball jersey with jeans, like, every day) and the number of v-ball clips on my Facebook page.

I'm finally shaking off the heartbreak, but I still feel stupid when I think of how, right before it went down, I was beaming like SpongeBob because I was genuinely happy for my then boyfriend. Picture gullible me, all chipper in the bleachers, watching Rick get honored as Peak Performance's Top Athlete in his age group. I jumped up and cheered so loudly when his name was announced that I gave myself laryngitis *and* a migraine. That was mere minutes before I found out that Rick had also worked on his playa-playa game during his summer away.

Yup, in August, Rick returned from camp with a new girlfriend—the hot v-ball star from a rival school. After practically skipping off the bleachers, intending to congratulate Rick and welcome him back with a kiss, I caught the sight of him hugging up on a Keke Palmer lookalike. He didn't even unglue himself from her when he saw me staring, frozen in shock. It didn't matter, because by then my voice was too hoarse (and my head too achy) to confront Rick.

We haven't spoken since.

But despite the prime-time shaft—witnessed by the entire athletic student body, by the way—I'm turning things around. It's October, and I've established myself as a new, strong player on Teawood High's varsity squad. Not even the sight of unslick Rick watching from the stands (with *her*) can throw off my game.

"London Abrams, you're on register." My manager's squawky voice yanked me back from my daydream.

I noticed that I'd been squeezing a helpless tube of paint, leaving it misshapen and crinkled. As best I could, I flattened it to its near-original figure before placing it at the back of the shelf behind the undamaged tubes.

My boss didn't notice—he's in his own world. While other managers and employees of Art Attack are funky, creative types, this one is offbeat in a chop-off-an-ear Van Gogh way. The poor guy seems tormented by a million unfinished personal art projects. He wears that torment in his hair. It looks more mad scientist than everyone else's bed-head vogue.

"*Great*, my favorite place to be," I said sarcastically, sidestepping his attempt at authority. With a million different possible payment transactions—cash, credit card, Art Attack bonuses, promotional codes, coupons, employee discounts, buy two get one half off deals—I still wasn't completely comfortable manning the checkout counter.

"Would you rather advise customers on how to put their art projects together?" he asked.

I suck at art advice. So, after stocking the shelves, I went to relieve the lanky goth guy signing off of register 1.

Fortunately for me, it was smooth sailing for the first two hours—just simple cash and credit card customers. But about a half hour before my lunch break, things started getting busy. The checkout lane signs—wide lamp shades displaying red numbers—blocked the shorter cashiers from view. On the flip side, my head towered above my lane's sign. Because they could see me, customers assumed I was the only employee on duty. So a long line formed at my register, while my coworkers at registers 2 and 3 seemed to be hiding behind their signs on purpose.

Just when I thought my boss would take notice of what was going on, an inquisitive customer whisked him away on a calligraphy ink hunt. It was up to me to handle the situation. I still had too much of that new-employee uneasiness to call out my coworkers, so I addressed the customers instead.

"Registers two and three are also open," I

informed the back of the coiling line.

My announcement totally backfired. A cutie had been heading to my line, but just as I said this, he queued up behind the two customers who had also just switched to register 2. *Dang.* Curious, I stole a quick glance at him. He struck me as a cross between a teenage Lenny Kravitz and a modern-day Jean-Michel Basquiat. (Yes, working here has taught me a thing or two about famous dead hipster artists.) Dressed in a plaid button-down and khakis, he looked retro and current at the same time.

In the two weeks that I'd been an Art Attack employee, I'd come to recognize the look of a person with creative swagger. And Kravitz Cakes's air of creativity was more timeless than most hot-for-the-moment, trendy customers who pass through. Something about him made me want to act supergirlie, like twirl my hair around my finger or tilt back my head while laughing. I think it's called "flirting."

I wanted to meet this guy. For one, he was taller than me—and possibly a full two inches taller at that. A lot of guys my age seem ten times more likely to catch mono than a growth spurt, so it's nice to come across a tall boy. Second—and this was huge—the mere fact that a guy caught my attention meant I must have been getting over unslick Rick.

I started ringing up customers at double speed. I couldn't move faster if my name was Taylor Swift. Forget the checkout counter small talk I'd normally have. I just wanted the cutie to switch back to my lane when he realized it was the quicker option.

Funny how total strangers operate on the same timetable without even realizing it. There were solid blocks of time when not a soul walked into Art Attack. Then suddenly, as if a sightseeing tour bus had pulled up and parked outside the door, folks swarmed in all around the same time.

My coworker at register 2 and I both had two customers waiting in line. The cutie was at the end of her line. As she rang up stuff, I stole a glance over my shoulder to her lane like a paranoid marathon runner. She had two more items to ring up—a roll of satin ribbons and a box of fancy transparent paper, apparently for a bride-to-be into DIY wedding invitations.

Yes, I thought. *Those items take mad long to ring up because the UPC has to be typed in.*

The two high-pitched beeps I heard in the next heartbeat meant that my coworker had somehow successfully managed to scan the wrinkled sticker codes on both packages. In a panic, I scanned my remaining three items and totaled the purchase. In a rare retail move (and without once removing his dark shades), my customer handed me glorious exact change.

The cutie looked over with anticipation when he noticed my now shorter lane. He took a step in my direction when, out of nowhere, a trio of loud Jersey types beat him to the punch. Only one of them was purchasing anything, but the obnoxious group made my lane look extra crowded.

"I *know*," one of the women heaved out in a raspy smoker's voice. "I would just *die-yah* if they had it—I'm *tawkin'* flat out *die-yah*."

Then, like a killer block at the net to save the game, my boss walked up and pulled through.

"We have that size of canvas panels you asked for in stock," he told the trio. "It'll be out in a few minutes if you want to wait for it."

The raspy-voiced woman was so excited,

she did almost *die-yah*. Her painful attempt to squeal with delight threw her into a coughing fit. Once she recovered, the excited group christened the store manager a *"dawll"* as he led them down a side aisle.

This time His Royal Hotness acted fast and moved to my lane just as I handed my outgoing customer his receipt. *Yes!* If daydreams could come true, I would jump over the Sharpie-marked counter into his waiting arms.

For all my effort to come face-to-face with him, I didn't think of anything clever to say to Mr. Crushtastic. I barely managed to greet him. He had such a quiet intensity that it felt like anything I said would've sounded silly. For one, he was as focused as I get when I'm on the court. Dude carefully examined each photo matting tool as he placed them on the counter. I recognized that need to concentrate on the details to get the job done right. I'm the same way when it comes to volleyball. And from what I could tell, this guy was heavy into his photography game.

The safest thing for me to do was ring him up in silence. Suddenly, I felt self-conscious and wished I hadn't worn my faded powder-blue jersey. It made my deep brown skin look totally washed out. Plus my Teyana Taylor thick, curly hair was wrestled into a messy ponytail as proof that I hadn't consulted the mirror enough while I styled it.

Fly Guy expected me to announce the grand total, but when I said nothing, he squinted at the glowing digital numbers on the register's screen. *Real smooth, London.* I wanted to throw the lamp-shade lane sign over my head and pretend I was a fixture. But for some reason, he was the one who looked embarrassed enough for the both of us. *Could I be making him nervous?* I wondered.

"Oh no," he said to himself, barely loud enough for me to hear. His stone-serious face softened into a grimace. "I'm short two bucks," he told me apologetically as he dug into his jeans pockets twice. "Uh . . . I could come back and pay you in two minutes, or I can just put something back and pick it up later . . . ," he rambled.

"No, it's okay," I heard myself say. "It's no biggie. I'll just use a promotional code and that should cover it." I made up what

I was saying as I went along. Meanwhile, my internal conversation went something like: *Why did I just decline his offers to swing by later? I just closed off my chance to see him again!*

"Thank you." He paused, looking at me as if for the first time. My stomach flip-flopped. The paper shopping bag I'd packed crinkled as he bashfully picked it up. Apparently our sudden stillness (and the sound of the bag) signaled to the waiting customer that it was time to ring up his manga artist brush-pen set and drawing pad. He slapped them onto the counter.

Nudged out, my crush turned away and walked out of the store.

Like a game-ending buzzer to a losing team, the door chime announcing his exit put me in a slight funk.

☆

"Earth to London." Pam waved her hands in front of my face. "*Gurl*, if you don't hurry up . . ."

I guess I had zoned out after the unidentified-fly-object-of-my-affection sighting.

When I finally snapped out of it, I moved from behind the counter to follow Pam. Her timing couldn't have been more perfect—I needed to step out for a break.

"I'll tell you the highlight of my morning," I answered, hoping my singsong voice piqued her curiosity. "This cu-TAY in *chief* got in my line when I was on register."

"Really, London?" Pam was touched, like I'd just handed her a bouquet of flowers. She couldn't hide her excitement over my interest in someone other than unslick Rick. There was something about Rick that she hadn't liked from the get-go. Pam has a sixth sense for these things and she picked up on Rick's superficial stench almost immediately. He cared too much about appearances for Pam's taste. That's an ironic opinion coming from a fashion *gearu* like herself, but it's more about her disgust over his obsession with status.

Pam's theory is that Rick only hangs with people he's *expected* to hang out with. (This is unacceptable to a girl who learned at a tender age to ignore the stares her mixed-race family sometimes got when out in public.) Case in point: Last year, when Rick was a newbie freshman volleyballer, he started dating me, a fellow newbie volley-baller. As soon as Rick was crowned Peak Performance's Top Athlete, he upgraded me for a star v-ball girlfriend. And ever since the Incident, Pam *really* can't stand even talking about him.

I for one am grateful Pam doesn't care about status. She befriended me in my unpopular middle school days. And now that I've been branded the "jilted girl-friend," she's just as supportive.

"You should've seen your gurl acting all crazy, speeding through customers so Fly Guy could slide over to my faster line," I confessed. "I still don't know what got into me. It was like I *had* to meet him."

"What's his name?" she asked the min-ute we claimed an unoccupied bistro table outside our favorite sandwich shop.

I couldn't conjure a juicy response if I'd wanted to. My involuntary facial expres-sions—primarily acted out by my dark, thick eyebrows—always snitch my true feelings. My eyebrows twitched and rose, then in the next millisecond, lowered. This reflex babbled to Pam that this was the end of my crush story. Nothing else to say.

"Well, at least you now know there's

crush life after Rick," she said before I could answer. "I'll go in and grab our lunch."

"Let me know if you need help carrying it out," I offered.

It had been only two weeks, but this was getting to be our Saturday afternoon ritual. And what made this ritual extra nice was finding a sweet lunch spot where we could people watch. For November it was a relatively warm day. Sitting in the sun would help us stay warm after we downed our cold soft drinks.

It was a great day for people watching. Lots of modely types were walking the Ave for some reason. The skater dudes hanging out near Starbucks were happy about that. Their jumps got riskier and more helter-skelter every time a group of girls walked by.

"It's mad busy out here," I commented as Pam and I ate. "I wonder what's going on today."

Sometimes, if the new bookstore was hosting an author signing, or if a performance at the arts center around the corner was poppin' off, there would be more foot traffic than usual. Pam shrugged and spotted someone interesting.

"He stays for*ever* framed out," she said

of the guy walking by in white-rimmed shades. For the many times we'd run into him, we'd never seen his eyes—rain or shine. "Lookin' like Kanye West in that ole 'Stronger' video," Pam continued.

"I'm sayin'," I agreed.

"Ooooh, come with me to Cynthea Bey's store," Pam pleaded, as if in response to something she told herself in her mind. She checked the time on her cell phone. "I wanna see what she came up with for the winter season."

Cynthea Bey had opened Chic Boutique—a cool warehouse space showcasing local and popular designer labels—a little over two months ago. Pam, the Cynthea groupie, had visited almost every week. I think she was stalking so she could one day cross paths with the supermodel. Despite her unlucky timing, Pam continued to have hope.

"We've got twenty-five minutes before I have to be back," I warned Pam. She's an overscheduling freak if you don't rein her in.

She hadn't even swallowed all of her food, but she stood up and threw away the rest of her sandwich and baby carrots. If I wasn't such a fast eater and hadn't already been done with my turkey baguette, there's no way I would have been leaving with her.

By the time we turned the corner toward Chic Boutique, the sight of a long line snaking from the store to the sidewalk twisted our faces into WTF grimaces.

"Are they giving away free clothes or something? What's with that crazy long line?" I asked out loud, but more to myself than to Pam. The last thing I felt like doing was dealing with a bunch of maniacal girls all vying for the same size-four jeans.

Pam and I stood staring in a paralyzed pause, reading the large pink storefront sign's swirly letters: CASTING CALL TODAY: 15 JERSEY GIRLS WILL BE SELECTED TO COMPETE FOR THE CHANCE TO BECOME *THE* CHIC BOUTIQUE MODEL IN OUR IN-STORE PRINT ADS!

It was clear that Cynthea Bey was out to prove that New Jersey could bleed style like New York. *Good for her,* I thought.

"I've seen enough." I tried to snap Pam out of her daze. I could tell she was excited. Nothing this huge had happened in Teawood since the year before when Jay-Z and Beyoncé were spotted buying iced coffees at the corner café. "Let's get out of here. I'm starting to catch a Rachel Zoe–clone contact high."

Pam didn't respond. "Quick, before I break out in an 'ohmygod' attack—or worse, break out in song." Still no response. "My humps. My humps. My lovely lady lumps."

Pam finally blinked; then she laughed at my rendition. "I'm sorry, this must be torture for you. I'll come back when this all blows over."

That's when I saw him. The hottie customer from Art Attack was just a few yards from me. He was talking to girls in the outdoor casting line. Even though most guys would love to have been in his position, it didn't seem like he was trying to hit on anyone. Instead, he looked professional—snapping digital shots of each contestant, then attaching printed photos onto forms he collected from every girl.

"That's him, that's him!" I whisper-screamed. Pam knew right away what and whom I was talking about. She followed the direction of my gaze to the object of my obsess—, er, affection.

He was as tall and calm as an oak tree. I wondered if that made me a pesky squirrel foraging for an acorn of his attention. It was nice to see him looking more relaxed than he had looked in Art Attack, where he'd gotten all bashful about coming up short. His former pocket-digging hands were now carrying a clipboard and a tiny camera. He pulled one of those cool portable photo printers from his back pocket.

The official-looking lanyard hanging around his neck confirmed that he wasn't loitering here to check out the girls. It also nicely topped off his intrepid reporter look. The only thing missing was a newsboy cap.

"What's he doing?" Pam asked.

Loverboy was holding his finger in the air, counting the heads of every girl in line outside. As he counted his way down and got closer to Pam and me, I was able to make out what was written in all caps on his lanyard: BRENT ST. JOHN, WWW.FACEMAG.COM, PHOTOGRAPHY INTERN.

That was when he reached us. He was mumbling numbers under his breath as he pointed at me and then finally Pam. "Twenty, twenty-one" I heard him say before he turned around and headed back to the first girl he had counted at the entrance of Chic Boutique. It seemed that there were also people standing inside the store who were being grouped in a separate head count.

"He thinks we're in line for this casting,"

I complained to Pam. *How did this happen?* I blamed it on the mesmerizing fuchsia store-front sign. We'd gotten caught up when we stood there frozen to read it. Now our absent-mindedness had made Fly Guy confused.

"This is a sign." A sudden gust of autumn wind blew Pam's flyaway strands into the sides of her mouth as she spoke excitedly. "You have to give him your number or something. Who knows if you'll ever meet him again? Much less twice in one day!"

He was about ten girls away from where we stood at the end of the line. I had to think fast. I had messed up the first time he and I were face-to-face. There had to be some way to strike up a conversation with him.

My inner scheming led me to the stack of applications jammed into a plastic brochure holder standing outside the door.

I grabbed one.

Pam knew where I was headed with this so she dug deep into her purse and furnished a pen. In the next hot minute, I was filling out the application as fast as I could.

Want to hear what the Romantic Comedies authors are doing when they are not writing books?

Check out **PulseRoCom.com** to see the authors blogging together, plus get sneak peeks of upcoming titles!

Sarah Mussi   Sarah Beth Durst   Nick Lake   Jessica Bendinger

Lit Up.

Get a taste of
our best-kept secrets.

New authors.

New stories.

New buzz.

A teen online sampler
from Simon & Schuster.

Available at
TEEN.SimonandSchuster.com

twitter.com/SimonTEEN

Margaret K. McElderry Books | Simon & Schuster Books for Young Readers | Simon Pulse
Published by Simon & Schuster

Amy Reed   Jessica Verday   Lauren Strasnick   Rhonda Stapleton

check YOUR PULSE

Simon & Schuster's **Check Your Pulse**
e-newsletter delivers current updates on
the hottest titles, exciting sweepstakes, and
exclusive content from your favorite authors.

Visit **TEEN.SimonandSchuster.com** to
sign up, post your thoughts, and find out what
every avid reader is talking about!

Margaret K. McElderry Books

Simon & Schuster
Books for Young Readers

SIMON PULSE